Advance Praise for *Apostle Islands*

"Like the miracles he depicts in *Apostle Islands*, Tommy Zurhellen's new novel is a gift of wonder and audacity. It is also deviously funny. Read it with his first novel, *Nazareth, North Dakota,* and consider yourself saved."

— Bruce Murkoff, author of *Red Rain* and *Waterbourne*

"Poignant, funny, and beautifully written, *Apostle Islands* is a big-hearted story and that rarest of books—a profound page turner. I loved it."

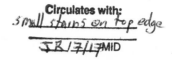

or of *Yoga Bitch*

"Tommy Zurhelle rime minister of zip. The geniu .ization of the upper Midwest ps the New Testament as surgical instrume this book anywhere, as you would the New Testament, and you'll come away startled, grinning and enriched."

— Djelloul Marbrook, novelist and award-winning poet

"Whether or not the biblical story of Jesus appeals to you religiously, Zurhellen's novels beautifully capture the human drama that makes good reading...Wonderful characters with clear compelling voices, each well worth getting to know."

— *Books, Personally*

Praise for *Nazareth, North Dakota*

"[T]his debut novel reveals the hardscrabble life of normal, unguided people who put their last dollars in the juke box and don't worry about what will happen when the song ends...Zurhellen's masterful dialogue often makes for gripping scenes that sustain these characters for decades."

—*Publishers Weekly*

"More than just a clever reimagining of the New Testament, *Nazareth, North Dakota* is an epic tale in its own right...[Zurhellen] demonstrates that while it may be true that there is nothing new under the sun, there's a good mix of enjoyment and insight to be found in recycling the old."

—*New York Journal of Books*

"[S]imply outstanding...This is the kind of book that will sit at the forefront of your mind for days..."

—NewPages.com

"Zurhellen takes the reader joy riding — in beat-up pick-up trucks and run-down vans and on marauding motorcycles — into familiar and surprising territory...where an old tale retold reminds us that the divine spark may yet be found under the most pedestrian of circumstances..."

—*Washington Independent Review of Books*

"[O]ne heck of a tale that's as much about the complexity of living in the modern world as it is about reinventing the icons of Christian tradition...an excellent book from a promising new voice in literature."

—*Small Press Reviews*

Apostle Islands[†]

† The Sequel to **Nazareth, North Dakota**

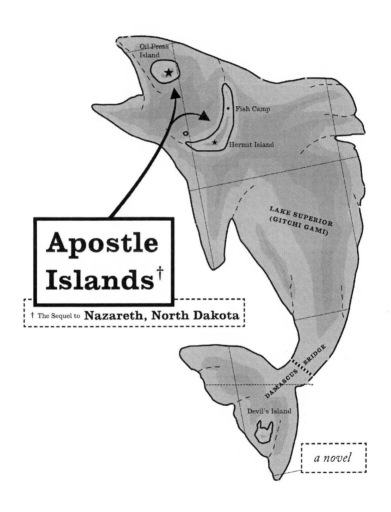

Oil Press
Island

Fish Camp

Hermit Island

Apostle
Islands†

† The Sequel to **Nazareth, North Dakota**

LAKE SUPERIOR
(GITCHI GAMI)

DAMASCUS BRIDGE

Devil's Island

a novel

TOMMY ZURHELLEN

An Atticus Trade Paperback Original

ATTICUS
BOOKS

Atticus Books LLC
13809 Oxmoor Place
Darnestown MD 20874
http://atticusbooksonline.com

ISBN-13: 978-0-9832080-9-9
ISBN-10: 0-9832080-9-3
Library of Congress Control Number: 2012943198

Typeset in Fairfield by David McNamara / sunnyoutside
Cover design by Jamie Keenan

Acknowledgments

First and foremost, thanks to Dan Cafaro for giving me the rare opportunity to continue this story; with his bare hands, he has created a press that truly matters, and that in itself is a literary miracle. Thanks also to his own apostles at Atticus Books, especially Lacey Dunham and Libby O'Neill, for their hard work and enthusiasm in seeing this project through. Congratulations to Jamie Keenan for designing two dazzling covers so good, they can walk on water.

Thanks to the Vermont Studio Center in Johnson, VT for granting me a second artist's residency to complete parts of this book. Thanks also to the following organizations for the generous use of their space and resources while writing and researching this book: the Bayfield Carnegie Library in Bayfield, WI; the Fargo Public Library in Fargo, ND; the Shipwreck Museum in Whitefish Bay, MI; the North Shore Commercial Fishing Museum in Tofte, MN; the Basilica of Mary Magdalene in Ste.-Maximin-La-Sainte-Baume; and the Blackwatch Library in Ticonderoga, NY.

A big ol' juicy-lucy of thanks to my friends Baker Lawley and Anna Drennen for allowing me to stay at Castle Danger while I scoured the Great Lakes a second time for artifacts, clues and conversations. Likewise, international thanks to

Jenny Hepburn and Peter McEldowney for their hospitality and endless London Pride while I stumbled to and from Marseille. Merci beaucoup!

Thanks to all my friends, colleagues and students who offered insight and encouragement for a second time around, especially Wendy Rawlings, Chris Settle, Josh Galitsky, Moe O'Donnell, Stevie "Guitar" Garabedian, Dr. Jimmy Snyder, Zayne Turner, Lea Graham, Robby Rob D'Ambrosio, and Nick Sweeney. And special thanks to Nicole "Strawberry Action" Hardy for the VSC coffee talks and Care Bear laughter.

Marquee thanks and gratitude go out to Robert, Linda, Ginny and Alex for their constant support.

And finally, Thanks Emeritus to Michael Martone and Ron Carlson, who showed me how this whole thing is done. I don't think *heroes* is too strong a word.

for Cha Cha
never an amateur

CONTENTS

O Mother, the doorway gives me a wicked smile;
What could do this to me—to be alone, a simple worker left with nothing?
In the deep, even old fish swim two-by-two through the sad sea
Fresh angels landed at Marseille yesterday morning
I hear the echoes of their distant song of death.
I am who am
Humble only because I have no worth

O Child, I've given you all I had;
Now get to work

—*Guillaume Apollinaire (1880–1918) "La Porte"*
(Translation from the French by Tommy Zurhellen)

Sermon on the Mount

Forget everything you know about heroes. Forget everything you learned as a little kid about fairy tales, too, because this is one story where the guy doesn't get the girl. Don't expect a pipe organ to play creepy music every time the villain walks into the room. Don't expect a fairy godmother to swoop down at the last minute and save the day with her magic wand, sashaying around shaking stardust in the air and singing *bibbity bobbity boo*. And don't expect to see some climactic battle scene, either, the kind where the hero fights some evil army of zombies, robots, genies, dragons, whiskey-drunk desperados, werewolves, wizards, carnivorous dinosaurs, sasquatch, smug corporate lawyers, secret agents, bloodthirsty pirates, politicians, beauticians, litterbugs, or little green men from Mars. Forget everything they taught you about true love; trust me, this ain't the kind of story with Fabio on the cover. No, the hero won't

be played by Johnny Depp in the movie adaptation. Don't
expect him to return in a sequel, because there is no sequel. This is it, the *denouement*, the final act where the
audience finds out if they've been watching a comedy or a
tragedy. Now if you're hoping for that ending where shiny,
happy people stroll off into the sunset, you got the wrong
guy. Forget everything you learned in school about how stories are supposed to end: sometimes the curtain can fall on
both a wedding and a funeral. Sometimes a story gets too
complicated to boil down to a simple choice between life
and death.

If you want a happy ending, sometimes the hero has to die.

I know what you're all thinking: I expected my messiah to be a little, you know, *taller*. You're thinking a messiah should have a name that sounds worthy of the Son of
God, not *Sam Davidson*, which sounds like your local car
mechanic or a shepherd or that goofy shop teacher from
sophomore year. You wanted a name with authority, something full of power and bravado like "Hercules McNinja" or
something sexy and dangerous like "Ace Diablo" or maybe
just plain old "Captain Omnipotent." You expected your
messiah to be good with a sword or a gun, or at least have
skills that'll matter most in a Battle Royale against Satan
and the forces of evil, skills like tae-kwon-do, deep-sea diving or making plastic explosives from a tube sock stuffed
with mayonnaise and motor oil. You expected an impossible whirlwind of MacGyver and Ozzy Osbourne and Obi
Wan Kenobi. You thought your messiah would be some kind

of cosmic rock star, bigger than the Beatles, someone who lives fast and dies young because like Def Leppard says: *it's better to burn out, than to fade away*. And then you met me. Right now, you're looking around this rocky hill on the lonely shores of Lake Superior and you're wondering why the hell you're all standing around an unemployed carpenter from North Dakota named Sam. You expected the salvation of the world to start someplace a little more picturesque than, you know, *Wisconsin*.

You're thinking, *holy shit*, this guy don't even speak in standard English.

You're thinking, the Messiah should *not* be quoting Def Leppard.

Truth be told, you all ain't exactly what I expected, neither. You people say you worry about salvation, but what you don't know about salvation could fill a hundred Lake Superiors. You worry so much about the *rules*. Now I'm no history scholar, but I do know a long time ago Moses came down from Sinai carrying the only ten rules that matter; and unless I'm mistaken, none of them got a problem with folks dancing too close, or using electricity, or leaving their ankles exposed; and no, the good book does not touch on blowjobs, or handjobs, or anything else they got drawn up in the *Kama Sutra*.

Believe me when I tell you, brothers and sisters: salvation is the oldest profession.

Listen: God will still love you if you eat bacon. He'll still want you if you smoke reefer or sleep with a complete stranger or download Motorhead onto your MP3. No, you ain't going to burn in hell if you use a condom. And My Father knows as well as anyone that in the right circumstances, sometimes vodka really is the only solution. You'll still get in the pearly gates of paradise if you say ugly words like *shit* or *fuck* out loud: believe me, a word can't be a curse if it ain't even a thousand years old. You want a real curse, just ask the Egyptians. *Locusts. Never-ending hail. A plague of blood.*

Death of the Firstborn, now that was a curse.

Forget everything you know about miracles. I can raise the dead, but I can't make you love me. I can walk on water, but these days all you've got to do is click on YouTube to see the impossible. We live in a world of too many miracles. We live in a world where people truly believe they can cheat death if they could just find the money to afford the right vitamin or surgical procedure.

Forget the odds. Listen, I know the math seems impossible: after all, there's more than seven billion people living on this earth, and only twelve of you.

I'm telling you to forget about the math. Forget grammar, too, because the revolution will not be determined by run-on sentences or dangling participles.

Forget about loyalty; in the end, one of you is going to betray me.

Remember all the things still worth fighting for in this crazy world, like kids on a slip n' slide or a happy dog slobbering on your arm. Remember everything good in this life, like driving with the top down while Steve Perry sings *don't stop believin'* or sitting at the bar at the VFW watching the old vets sip Bud Light and tell each other whoppers.

Remember that in this world, there's no such thing as a true story: we're all human, and we're all liars. We are all storytellers, and we all create our own fairy tales. We forget we can all change the story, because we *are* the story. Remember we are good *and* evil. We are right *and* we are wrong. Remember that in the end, we have to be the heroes as well as the villains.

Remember me, because in this story, even the Gods have to die.

The Wedding at Cana

Spring 2011

I wake up in the car with someone waving a gun in my face and I'm thinking, *this is going to be one fucked up wedding*. Clearly it's not going to be the kind of wedding with invitations, which is good, because I don't have one. And it's not the kind where people wrap presents in fancy white paper or drink champagne, either, while a string quartet covers Coldplay or Kool & The Gang. This is going to be the kind of wedding where the music comes from whoever's got the baddest pickup: Skynyrd, Trace Adkins, Ted Nugent. It's going to be the kind where the women bring ham salad, the dudes bring their dogs and everyone shouts "Free Bird!" The kind where folks bring their own wine. I know all this because back where I come from in North Dakota, it's probably the only kind of wedding a girl is going to get. But I didn't drive all the way out here just to sit through another tailgate jamboree.

I'm here because I'm a girl who is tired of waiting around.

I'm curled up in the backseat with my head buried in a makeshift pillow when a guy dips his head in the driver's side window and pokes at me with a little hip-pocket .22. My eyes are still half-shut but I know it's a guy from the smell of bar soap and sweat. The gun doesn't scare me much; when you work enough nights at the Flying J you get your fill of drunk truckers pulling pistols out of their pants and wagging them in the air like winning lottery tickets. And to be honest, I just spent nine hours in the car with Laz to get here, so if there's a choice between a gun in my face or listening to my brother speak French for five hundred miles, oh Sweet Lord, I'm taking the gun every time.

Besides, I'm also a girl who keeps her own gun under the pillow.

The first thing this guy says to me is, "You're a woman." He sounds surprised. He's got a squeaky little voice and with my eyes still shut, I'm picturing an accountant or some nerdy clerk, that squirrelly little guy in the movies with big glasses who's always bothered about something.

"Thanks for the update," I say, face still sunk into the jacket I've rolled up into a lumpy pillow. "You mind pointing that thing somewhere else?" After a moment, I can hear him and his gun slowly drawing back out of the driver's side window.

"Well, you sure don't *look* like no damn federal agent."

I slowly sit up. "Just how many federal agents you find asleep out here?" I'm wondering where in the hell Laz has gone off to; I figure if he's got himself shot, all the complaining would've woken me a long time ago. I rub the sleep out of my eyes with my right hand; the left's still on the jacket. I'm ready to give this little gun-toting peanut a piece of my mind when I finally get a good look at him.

That's when I let out a nice, polite *Holy Shit*.

This guy has to be close to seven feet tall, and about as wide as a couple of washing machines roped together. All I can really see in the window is his belt buckle. When he bends back down he reminds me of a grizzly bear checking out a beehive. Now I can see his face: he's young, probably about twenty-two, with a patchwork beard and big freckles on his face. He's wearing overalls with no shirt, and his bare biceps look like a couple of canned hams hanging off his shoulders. And although I never read the book, suddenly I know exactly how all those little people in *Gulliver's Travels* felt when they woke up and found a giant dude walking around their world.

We look each other over for a moment, but from his easy smile I get the gut feeling he's not a bad guy. Which is a good thing, because I also get the feeling he could crush this car with his bare hands.

He rubs the boyish scruff on his chin, still trying to figure me out. "You some kind of reporter, then?"

I stretch out my arms and yawn. "Do I look like a reporter?" The morning sun is coming through the windshield, making me squint. I have to pee. "There's a wedding around here today, right?"

He nods. "I'm kind of helping out with security," he says. "You invited?"

I hold out my hand in a see-saw. "Kind of. You know Sam Davidson?"

He perks up. "Hell, everyone knows Sam."

"Yeah, well," I say, taking the deepest breath I can manage before my first cigarette of the day. "I'm his girl."

The smile disappears, and he cocks his head sideways. "Sam Davidson ain't got no girl," he says, his voice now stiff like he just caught me shoplifting gum. "What's your name?"

When I tell him, the warm smile slowly appears again. "You're Daylene?" He bangs the roof of the car with his palm. "Hot damn. What the hell you doing sleeping out here?"

"I guess this is what you'd call a surprise entrance." I lick my dry lips and get my first good look at where I parked last night; things look different at three in the morning. I see we're in the middle of some kind of meadow about fifty feet off the main road. For once I'm glad I listened to the GPS: another hundred yards and I'd have driven straight into Lake Superior. The water looks calm and shiny in the morning sun, and for a moment it reminds me of California. I lift my hand from the pillow to run it through my tangled hair, but as soon as I do I remember what I did in the bathroom before we left Bismarck. There's probably a rule against taking clippers to your hair right before a road trip, but I remember looking in the mirror and thinking, *what the hell, Daylene, you're twenty-eight years old and it's almost summertime and short hair can be really sexy on a road trip.*

Right now, I'm thinking it better look sexier than it feels. God, it's like I joined the Navy.

"Sam talks about you a lot," the giant says. "You don't look at all like I pictured."

"Yeah, well," I say. "You don't look much like a security guard to me."

He leans back, tugs on his overalls. "You're right about that. No, this is just something I picked up for the weekend. I'm really trying to break into wrestling."

"You don't say," I mumble, not doing a very good job of sounding interested. I picture him getting in the ring and grappling with an opponent more his size, like a blue whale or maybe a freight train.

"My name's Johnny," he says, his voice getting more excited. "Me and my brother Jimmy, we're a tag team. We go by the name The Sons of Thunder," he says, and when he gets to *The Sons of Thunder* it echoes like on those old monster truck show commercials. "Sam actually gave us that name—on account of we both make a lot of noise, I guess." He scratches his forearm. "We used to go by The Drunken Cossacks, but my Russian accent really sucks. You ever heard of us?"

"Can't say I have," I say. "But we don't hear much of anything over in North Dakota."

"Well, we're getting pretty big. We've got a match against Devil and Ms. Jones down in Green Bay this weekend, you should come check it out."

"Well, I'm definitely planning on sticking around," I say, but I'm a little distracted; I'm still relishing the warm glow on my face from when this guy said *Sam talks about you a lot.* Maybe this road trip wasn't a bad idea after all. Okay, now I really have to pee. "Wait, *Ms.* Jones? You're fighting a woman?"

"Not exactly," he says. "Ms. Jones dresses up like a woman, but he weighs about 450 pounds. The Devil is this skinny little dude with a moustache who dresses up like—well, you know." He turns to spit into the tall grass. "Didn't mean to scare you before, Daylene. Got my orders, is all. Supposed to be on the lookout for any kind of government agent."

I look around again at the empty meadow. "Exactly what kind of agents are you expecting out here?"

He scratches the shaggy hair under his worn John Deere ball cap. "All kinds I guess: FBI, ATF, State Police. We see Border Patrol trucks now and then, on account of that's Canada over there," he says, pointing north across the water. "Lately we even got some pencil-neck from the IRS snooping around. That's what I hear, anyway," he says, pulling his cap down over his eyes. He spits again and smiles. "When the Surgeon General shows up, I'm done."

"God bless Homeland Security." Now I'm worried; Sam had mentioned something on the phone about a little trouble with the law last time we spoke, but he didn't make it sound that serious. Typical Sam. Hearing it from this guy, it sounds more like another Ruby Ridge. This makes me want to know who he's been hanging around with these last few months; it sure as hell hasn't been the Make-A-Wish Foundation or the Wisconsin chapter of the goddamn Boy Scouts of America.

"All the same, sure is a pretty place to have a wedding," Johnny says wistfully, pointing through some trees that line the edge of the meadow. "You can see the lighthouse through there. That's state park, but this here's private property. That's why I poked in on you."

"Sorry, I guess everything looked the same at three in the morning." I have to admit, the place does look a lot different with the sun up. Even through the dirty windshield, I can see it's really a beautiful spot.

There's still no sign of Laz anywhere. When big Johnny finally says goodbye and leaves me alone, I search around the floor for my cell phone. I find it under an empty Doritos bag; it's been off most of the way, since the battery's been low ever since we made Minnesota. When I turn it back on there's a voice message—but it's not Laz, it's from Roxy, calling last night to ask if me and Laz wanted to crash at her motel room in town.

I rub my aching back and think, *great timing.*

I search around for my smokes and listen to the message a second time, paying close attention to Roxy's voice. She sounds drunk again. I curse under my breath: Sam's not going to like his mother showing up at this thing half in the bag. I'm just about to call Laz when he finally pops his head in the window, surprising me. "Where the hell have you been?" I say.

"Taking a walk," he says. "What happened over here? It looked like you were getting mugged by the Incredible Hulk."

"Thanks for coming to my rescue, big brother." I heave myself off the backseat and push the driver's seat forward so I can reach the door handle. "I'm fine, by the way."

As usual, he ignores me. He's too busy breathing in the morning air like he's standing on the deck of a cruise ship or something. "*A bon santé, ma soeur.*"

"Swear to God," I say, swinging the door open and banging it on his knee. "Start with the French again and I'm calling the Hulk back."

Laz steps back to let me out. He puts his hand under his shirt to rub his ribs. "When does this wedding start anyway? I'm getting hungry."

I touch the screen on my cell. "We got about six, seven hours."

"Not good, not good. Definitely need breakfast, then," he says, suddenly turning to look at me with a raised eyebrow. "And what are you planning to wear?"

Honestly, in the rush to get in the car back in Bismarck, I didn't think much about that. "Didn't pack much," I say, looking at the swamp of assorted junk stuffed inside the car. I lean over and put my face on the window. "Got a clean T-shirt in there someplace."

"Are you kidding?" he says. "Come on Cinderella, we have to get you ready for the ball. There's bound to be a town around here with the essentials: coffee, cigarettes, and a nice summer dress. Move aside, I'll drive." He stands firm in front of the door and holds out his hand for the keys. There's this flash of excitement in his voice that I don't hear that much. "Daylene, come on. You haven't seen Sam in months. If you're going to cut your hair like Sinead O'Connor, at least wear something nice."

I forgot about my hair. "It's not that bad."

"You look like one of the lost boys from *Peter Pan*."

"Why do you care?" I yell, but I stomp around to the passenger seat; wherever we stop, it'd better have a bathroom. "In fact, remind me why you're here at all." I get in and dig my sandals into the dirty floorboard.

Laz shrugs his boney shoulders. "I like being part of a love story."

"Ha, ha," I say. "This ain't no love story."

He purses his lips and lets out a fat raspberry. "Oh, really? What is it then?"

"If I knew," I say, reaching on the dash for my sunglasses. "I'd tell you."

He starts the car and pulls us out onto the gravel road. He's driving like a teenager trying to pass his road test, checking the mirrors a dozen times. I'm pretty sure he never bothered to get his license back after his last stint at James River, but I'll need at least one cup of coffee before I can start another argument. I should be nervous with him behind the wheel, but it feels nice not to be the one driving for a change. I slip on my Jackie O shades and lean back. He taps his finger on the GPS screen a few times and we're off, headed down this windy gravel road towards some town called Cape Ernum.

As I settle back into the seat, my eyes get heavy. I feel like I could sleep for another week. When I'm not looking he manages to change the woman's voice on the GPS from English to French.

I already know in my heart this won't turn out to be a love story. Sure, it's got all the elements: there's a girl, there's a boy. There's the cute meet: boy sits next to girl on a bus back in high school to prevent girl from strangling some vile harpy named Kathy Jubilee. But now it's ten years later and the girl is pushing thirty. The ending of the story is still up in the air, but today the girl woke up alone in the back of a Ford Fiesta somewhere in bumfuck Wisconsin, so prospects don't look all that good.

I wish I knew the difference between any old story and a love story. It's more than just love, I can tell you that much. Some people tell you love means sacrifice, but I hope to God there's more to it than that. I sure as hell don't want to end up some martyr with the life sucked out of their bones, like Roxy. I want a life full of skinned knees and good wine and a kitchen that smells like roasted garlic and coffee. I want home cooked meals full of saturated fat. I want *gravy*. I want porch swings and sloppy dogs on your lap and laughter. I want a life that's not afraid to waste time on all the dumb things like big earrings, birthday cake, petting zoos, getting stranded on top of the Ferris wheel, holding hands in the dark. I want to dress up like Cleopatra for costume parties. I want to go skinny-dipping with my man because it's Wednesday. Basically, I want the impossible love story:

the one where Sam and I grow old together. The one I know damn well I won't get.

Listen to yourself, Daylene, you sound like a child: *I want, I want, I want, I want.*

But Sweet Lord, I've waited ten years for this. I'm not going back: today is the day I'm going to tell him, this girl is sticking around no matter what. Today is the day I make things crystal clear: this is a girl who is not going home. This is a girl who has paid her dues.

So, damn right *I want.*

Starting today I'm the fucking Queen of Want.

Leave it to Laz to pull up in front of the one café in this two-horse town with no sign, half a wagon wheel dangling in the window and a long row of motorcycles parked out front. The only way I'm sure it's a café and not a tractor supply or a pool hall is the smell of bacon and home fries wafting across the street when we get out of the car. "It's got that rustic charm," he says, like he found it in the Michelin guide.

"I don't need rustic charm," I say. "I just want coffee."

Cape Ernum droops down to the water from a steep hill. The air smells like pine needles and old fish, and this early in the morning there are more sea birds standing on the sidewalks than people. In a weird way, it reminds me a lot of Nazareth—but then again, all small towns have certain things in common: same sleepy streets, same dusty mom-and-pops. Same dirty secrets that folks take to their graves.

A couple of the bikers stand on the curb, watching us get out of the car through their dark wraparound shades. They look like they've been standing there since the 1960s: scraggly hair, dusty jeans, big black boots, permanent scowls on their faces. They're wearing these denim vests over their shirts that have some kind of insignia sewn into the back. When we get closer to the door I can get a better look: in the middle there's a picture of a wavy dagger with a snake wrapped around it. Above the dagger is a crescent of big letters that reads SICARII and below it reads CAPE ERNUM. I don't know what *Sicarii* means, but the whole snake-and-dagger-thing gives me the creeps. They both turn and stare some more as we pass by. Laz has this look on his face like he's sorry he stopped here. One of them grunts at us like a water buffalo.

Right now I'm sorry I left my gun in the backseat.

Inside the café is crowded; there's got to be a dozen of these biker dudes along the counter and a few more into a back booth. They're noisy as children, and when we walk in they all turn and look at us at the same time, like we're from the circus or Mars or New York City or something. I notice the same wavy dagger tatt on a lot of their forearms. The only empty booth is right next to the front door, so I slide in and push the dirty dishes to the edge. Laz is still standing there like he's searching for the best table in the house.

"Sit down," I whisper. "What the hell are you looking for?"

"I feel like I'm in *The Wild One*," he says, and unless everyone at the counter is stone deaf, they hear every word. "I'm looking to see if one of them is Marlon Brando."

I sink my head down and pitch a menu in front of my face. I will say this about my brother: for such a skinny dude, he is fearless. I've seen him talk his way out of just about everything: muggings, bar fights, pissed-off cops, pissed-off dealers. One time back in Bismarck these five frat boys from BSU were about to kill him—for what I don't know, probably just being gay—but after twenty minutes of Laz talking and joking and slapping backs, these dudes are buying him sweet potato fries at Dakota Farms. He sure can talk, I'll give him that; when he wanted to come on this trip I figured he might be good in a jam. But right now I'm doing the math and there are twenty-six of these bikers in here and only two of us. I want to call Sam on my cell as a last resort—but in a weird way, that feels even more scary right now. Especially since I haven't quite figured out how to tell him I'm here.

Laz finally dumps himself into the seat across from me and inspects the stained plastic-coated menu. A waitress shows up to take our order and clear the dishes. Her nametag reads *June*. She's a thin old gal with greying pigtails and pink running shoes; around her nametag is a constellation of buttons in loose orbit that say things like *On the Seventh Day, God Went Fishin'* and *You Want to Catch'Um, You Got to Ernum*. From the way she grinds her bubble gum I can tell she's been waiting tables a lot longer than me. I'm guessing she's no more than forty but there's something behind her eyes that tells me she's racked up more than her share of mileage.

"Do you have crème brulee?" Laz says, tapping at the menu. "I don't see it here."

I try to kick him under the table, but I miss him and bang my toe on the bench instead.

"That's a dessert, right?" she says, not missing a beat. She smacks her gum. "I can give you a piece of pie. That's a dessert."

"Now *that* sounds good," he says. "Do you have apple?"

"Best damn apple pie in Jericho County," she says, jotting on her pad before turning to me with her hound dog look. "And you, sweetie? Let me guess—crepes suzette."

"Just coffee," I say. "Black."

"Oh, get her a piece of the apple, too," Laz says, waving his hand like the three of us are old friends. "She needs the energy today."

"Two pies and a coffee," June says. "Now I can retire."

After she leaves, I slip into the ladies room. I try not to look at my hair in the mirror when I'm washing my hands. When I come back, Laz is playing with everything on the table: the salt and pepper shakers, the sugar, the ketchup. He picks them up and puts them back down. He does this a lot. Sometimes it's hard to believe my brother's thirty-five years old; it's even harder to believe he's been to prison three times. I sit back down and pretend to watch the street but I'm keeping a sharp eye on the counter; I can hear these biker guys talking about us. "Those guys are talking about us," I say.

"They seem all right. Are you sure they're talking about us?"

I lean forward and whisper to him. "Unless two other people came in who answer the description *half-pint and the skinny homo*, yeah, I'd say I'm sure."

I've never defended myself with a butter knife, but there's always a first time.

Laz doesn't seem to care much, but at least he's finally stopped messing with everything on the table. "When June comes back, ask her if she knows a good dress shop in town."

"Ten bucks says she never comes back at all, thanks to you." But as soon as I say it, she returns with the pie and coffee. She wasn't kidding about the pie; it's flaky and fat with chunks of fruit. The coffee's what I expect: shitty and weak, like all diner coffee. But it's still coffee, and since I'm supposed to be giving up smoking, this might be all the help I get today.

Laz is already licking his plate. "This is the pie they serve in heaven."

I'm on my second cup of the coffee they serve in hell when out of the corner of my eye, I spot one of the bikers push away from the counter and come towards our booth. I notice a diamond stud in his ear and that same wavy dagger tattoo on his forearm; the blade is pointing inwards, and it's so long the tip disappears under his T-shirt. But my intuition tells me the haircut and smile on this guy are all wrong for a biker; if you stuck a nice suit and tie on him, he could run for governor.

He's good-looking I guess, in an evil genius sort of way.

"My spies tell me you're Daylene Hooker," he says with a grin. He's checking his iPhone while he's talking; he's got this smooth voice that a hundred years ago probably was perfect for selling snake oil or the Brooklyn Bridge. "Am I right?"

I take my time, staring out the window at this teenage girl pushing a stroller down the sidewalk. Laz is oblivious as he finishes up my pie. I take another lazy sip of my coffee before I look up at the stranger. "Your spy wouldn't happen to wear overalls and be the size of a woolly mammoth, would he?"

He laughs. "So you've met Johnny Thunder." He puts out his free hand; I notice the ring on his finger is wrong too, a big graduation sparkler that reads *University of Michigan*. "My name's Judd Sackett. Good friend of Sam."

I reach out to shake his hand, slowly at first, like this is a test I haven't had enough time to study for. Right away I don't like him, although for the life of me I can't say exactly why; I know plenty of cool bikers back at the Flying J, so it's not that. "This is my brother, Laz."

"Nice to meet you both. Welcome to Cape Ernum."

The waitress comes back to take the plates and top off the coffee. When she leaves, Judd watches her go, waiting a moment before speaking again. He keeps clicking away at his phone while he talks. "That's June," he says, jerking his head in her direction as she disappears into the kitchen. "She catches fish in her sleep. Husband does, too."

"Can I ask you a question?" I say, stirring my cup. "What does *Sicarii* mean?"

For some reason, Laz figures this is the time for him to finally pipe up. "It's Latin. Plural of *Sicarius*. Literally, I think it means 'dagger-men.'"

"I'm impressed," Judd replies, still typing. "You must be a professor or something."

Laz blushes like he's accepting an Academy Award. "Oh, you have no idea."

"Dagger-men," I say, still stirring. "So like, assassins."

Judd shrugs his shoulders. "We like to think more like, *patriots*. After all, freedom does have a price," he says, like this is a lecture hall. "George Washington certainly agreed with that."

"George Washington never wore a snake and a knife on his back."

"You got me there," he says, trying to laugh it off. "Listen, I don't want to get off on the wrong foot. After all, friends of Sam are our friends." As he's talking, one of the other bikers comes and whispers something into his ear. Judd nods and sends him away. "Hey, the boys are about to head over to the lighthouse and pull the cork on a new batch of corn wine we made for the wedding. Why don't you join us?"

"Bit early for drinking, ain't it?" I pull some bills out of my pocket for the table.

Laz perks up with the word *wine*. "Now that sounds good. I'm actually a bit of a White Lightning connoisseur myself."

"Really," Judd says, laughing. "You drink a lot of the lightning, do you?"

"Only in prison," Laz says. "Back at James River we called it something else."

Suddenly, Judd is interested. He puts his phone down and turns to give my brother a better look. "You've done time?"

Laz smiles and leans forward on the table, looking down the row of dudes at the counter. "Haven't we all, gentlemen?"

"James River is a bad joint," Judd says, rubbing his chin. "What were you in for?"

"Distribution," Laz says. "And—"

"And *now* he's on the straight and narrow," I say, standing up and pulling on Laz's arm. "Nice to meet you all, see you at the wedding."

When we're outside, Laz slips my arm. "Thanks for the insult, little sister," he says, acting all blustered. "*Narrow* I get, because I'm thin and trim—but *straight*? Please," he says. "Not on your life."

"Shut up and get in the car."

"But we haven't found you a dress yet." He looks around the street, using his hand to shield his eyes from the sun with a dramatic flair, like he's suddenly scouting for Lewis and Clark. "*Voila*, there's some kind of boutique," he says, pointing down towards the waterfront. "Should be open by now."

"I don't think dress code is going to be a problem at this thing," I say, looking back at the window of the café. "If gang colors are okay, I guess my T-shirt will pass."

"Make you a deal," he says. "You come with me to look at dresses for ten minutes, and I won't talk about it ever again. That, or the hair. My lips are sealed."

I stare at him, still smoldering.

"Okay, enough pouting," he says. "It's obvious you need help—a Laz-ervention, if you will. You need a cold shower and some air conditioning, right away. Now think: who else is coming to this wedding? Don't we know someone who's got a motel room we can barge in on?"

"I could call Roxy," I say half-heartedly. "She left a message."

He claps his hands. "There we go," he says. "Call her back. We'll find you a dress, then head over. We're going to have a good time, you'll see. You'll get to see Sam, and after a couple glasses of wine you'll feel even better, trust me."

I put my hand on his shoulder. "Do me a favor, stay away from the wine they serve at this thing."

"It might be good," he says.

"Good on stains, maybe." Some of the biker dudes come out of the café and hover around their motorcycles. They're staring at us, or maybe it just feels like they are. "And while you're at it, stay away from that Judd guy, too. I don't trust him."

I take out my cell and scroll down to Roxy's number. Granted, I have no idea which Roxy is going to pick up, but

I'm tired and dirty and cranky and I'm willing to take my chances.

The wine they bring to a wedding like this really isn't wine at all; it's more like a second cousin to kerosene. I guess they call it *wine* because calling it moonshine will get you arrested. Back in NoDak the old timers put it in pickle jars and call it prairie poison, but I've heard folks call it white lightning, apple jack, corn wine, pruno, potato sweat, mountain dew. It's all the same: you take a bunch of fruit or vegetables, boil the holy hell out of it, add some sugar and baker's yeast, and let it sit in the basement for six months or so. Then you pour it through a paper towel into some old jugs and *wham*, you've got yourself a Saturday night. Or a wedding. Some folks cut it with a few packets of Kool Aid to make it go down easy, but drink enough of that stuff and sooner or later, you'll go blind. Back in Naz, when you saw an old man sitting on a porch with a cane and dark glasses, you knew it wasn't some birth defect.

I look at Roxy now and I see an old woman gone blind.

Sweet Lord, I used to look at her and think to myself, *that's my hero.* Wasn't so long ago I wanted to be just like her. I'd never get tired listening to her tell stories about Sam when he was young, or about Joe when he was alive. She could spin some whoppers, and God, how I loved her for it. I can still remember the first time we met, in the supermarket back in Nazareth. She was so beautiful; back then she always wore this smile like she knew the score. I know she's had more pain and loss in her life than I can imagine since then; she lost her husband, and I still don't even know how the man died. Now she's losing her son. She lives alone in that big old house back in Naz, with Joe's old pickup still parked in the front, gathering weeds. Every time I pass the house I feel like I'm passing some old forgotten graveyard.

But me and Roxy have the same problem: we both love a man who is going to die.

The steering wheel feels like it's going to come loose in my hands; I don't know the speed limit because there's no signs out here—but whatever it is, right now we're doubling it. The car is bouncing around like we're inside a dishwasher and the GPS lady is yelling at me in French. Laz is translating her droning voice from the passenger seat but it's hard to hear either of them, since we lost the muffler about a mile back to a big rock sticking out of the dirt. The AC has decided to work so with the windows up, it sounds like we're trapped inside a popcorn machine. I'm pretty sure one of the tires is about to rattle loose, but I can't stop now. I stomp on the gas harder.

We're late for this wedding.

"Honestly, I didn't know the Fiesta could go this fast," Laz shouts in my ear, his arms hugging his legs to his chest in the crash position. "I know the speed dial goes to a hundred, but I always thought that was just for show."

Rest my eyes, my ass. I should've known better than to lie down on the plastic couch in Roxy's motel room, even for a minute. We called Roxy on her cell and she said she'd already left for the wedding, but we could definitely crash there for a few hours. When we get there, I convince myself I'll close my eyes for fifteen minutes; when I open them again suddenly it's the middle of the afternoon and Laz is on the floor in front of the bed, watching *I Love Lucy*. Then I'm rushing around the room trying to get ready, yelling at him at regular intervals for not waking me up. Laz keeps going on about how it's a special case because it's the episode where Lucy gets wasted on vegetable tonic while she's doing a TV commercial, so it's not his fault.

We take another hard turn on the dirt road and I can finally see the lighthouse looming in the distance, its windows at the top reflecting the bright midday sun. "You should've tried harder to wake me up."

"Trust me, I *did* try. The only thing left was sticking your hand in the wall socket."

"We missed the ceremony," I say, trying to concentrate on the road. "Sure, we don't even know the bride and groom at this thing, but there has to be some kind of rule about missing the *wedding* part of a wedding."

"So we missed the boring part," he says. "Don't be mad at *me*."

"I'm not mad at you for that," I say. "I'm mad at you for making me buy this dress." I look down at this thing I have on, a drunken swirl of hot pink and toilet bowl blue that's got some kind of farm animal pattern all over it: cows, geese, horses, pigs tilting back and forth like drunken footballs. I didn't have time to shave, either, so from the waist down I know I probably would pass for Bigfoot's baby sister.

"It's a conversation starter. And it smells a whole lot better than what you had on."

"It's hideous," I say. "If Old MacDonald had a whorehouse, this would be the drapes."

The road starts to look familiar again from this morning. When we clear the last bend before the entrance to the park, I see four or five police SUVs parked on both sides of the road right in front of us. I stomp on the brake with both feet, but there's no way they missed us coming around that turn at demolition-derby speed. I'm ready to pull over and find my license and have a good, sappy story ready, but when we slowly roll by the line of trucks none of them seem to care much; they sip at their iced coffees and nod to us as we pass by.

"That's weird," I say as we pass through the big stone arch of the park. "What the hell are so many of them doing out here, anyway?" I remember what Johnny Thunder told me when I woke up this morning.

"Reminds me of the opening scene of *The Godfather*," Laz says. "You know, where the feds sit outside Don Corleone's wedding, taking down license plate numbers." He thinks about it for a moment and smiles. "Marlon Brando, for the *second* time today. Now that's weird."

I pull into the makeshift parking lot and wedge the Fiesta between two huge pickups. There's a dog tied up in the back of one that starts yapping at us. There are probably a hundred or so cars and trucks out here now; the place looks a lot different than this morning. Most of the plates are Wisconsin but I spot a couple Michigans and Minnesotas, too. I cut the engine but don't get out of the car; I just sit there with my hands on the wheel. Laz is talking—when is he not?—but right now, I'm not listening to a word.

I'm going over what I want to say to Sam.

I want, I want, I want.

Somewhere between this parking lot and that lighthouse over there, I will find the guts to tell him he'd better get used to the Queen of Want around here. It might be tough getting him alone: nothing against the beautiful couple of this wedding, but I'd bet most of these cars are here more to listen to Sam, and less to hear the *I Do's*.

"Look at all these people," I say, shaking my head. "I love Sam, but I hate the crowds."

"You don't hate crowds," Laz says, getting out of the car. "You just hate weddings."

"That's not true," I blurt out. My stomach lurches into an old knot. "That's not fair, Laz."

I figure it'll take hours to find Sam in this giant amoeba of a crowd, but it turns out I don't have to wait at all: the first thing I see when I get out of the car is Sam. I can't miss him: I know I'm biased, but he's the dreamy one coming right towards me. He must have seen my car pull in. I notice his chestnut hair is longer and bleached from too much time in the sun. He's grown a bit of scruff on his face now, too, and even from a distance I notice a few more stress lines on his face. He sees Laz first and gives him a big hug.

I don't know what to think about all the dudes.

As usual, there's this semi-circle of dudes following Sam at a distance, like waterskiers tied behind a boat. Most of them I've never seen before; I only recognize Phil and Nate from the old days in Nazareth, and we nod at each other.

Something tells me Sam is always going to be surrounded by bunches of dudes.

"You look beautiful," he says to me.

"You're just saying that," I say. "This dress is a train wreck."

"You're still beautiful. You cut your hair."

I touch his face. "And you're growing a beard."

"You like it?"

"I'll let you know," I say. "It takes a lot of research for a girl to decide."

Sam takes my hand and squeezes it. "I'm really glad you came," he says, and in an instant everything about this cursed voyage to Wisconsin is worth it: the nine-hour drive, the French, the lost muffler, even this drunken barnyard of a dress. I still feel the electricity of his touch, and I'm so happy to see him—but I have to say, it's hard to get close to your man with a dozen or so of these Dudes-in-Waiting watching from about twenty feet away. In their Tevas and Rockports and lumberjack shirts, they look like the hippie Secret Service.

"How's your mom?" I say. "I talked to her this morning and she sounded like—well, she might have started the party early." I never know what to say about Roxy these days.

Sam's face sinks to a frown. "Roxy is Roxy," he groans. "She's already here somewhere, but honestly, I don't know what to say to her anymore."

I squeeze his hand back, and just when I think it's the perfect moment to drag Sam away and say all the things I want to say, here comes the Dagger-Man from the café this morning. This Judd character walks right up to Sam, as if I'm not standing *right here*. "Sam, there's some people just came in from the UP who can't wait to meet you," he says. "Spare a minute?"

Sam's arm is around my shoulders now and he gives me a little squeeze. "Have you two met?"

"We ran into each other in town," I say, folding my arms. "We share a love of pie and George Washington."

"Absolutely," Judd says. "Sam, it'll only take a minute."

Sam grumbles and puts his hands in the air. "Daylene, I—"

"Honey, I understand," I say, pushing gently on his chest. "Save me a dance, though. I've got things I need to talk to you about."

"Good things?"

I bite my lip, and then nod. "The best."

Sam heads off towards the lakeshore. Judd turns to follow him, but after a couple steps he stops and faces me, checking to make sure Sam and the Dude Parade are out of range before he says anything to me. "Can I ask you a question, Daylene?"

"Sure," I say, but I already know exactly what he wants to ask me. It's the same question I've been asked for the last ten years, the one I get every time someone tries to get close to Sam. It's probably impossible for me to say how I feel about other people getting close to Sam without sounding like a complete bitch, so I'll simply say that to me, this guy is just an amateur.

He rubs his chin. "All I've heard this morning is about Daylene Hooker. So I guess my question is, how well do you know Sam?"

That's not the question he wants to ask, but I answer it anyway. "Oh, pretty well."

I reach back into the car to grab my sunglasses off the dash. The Dude Convoy has already left to tail Sam and my brother is long gone, so right now we're alone. Somewhere in the parking lot a truck starts blaring Van Halen and it only takes a second before everyone down by the water whoops to the song at once. I can hear some guy yell *Have You Seen Junior's Grades?* at the top of his lungs, but he's got the wrong song. No one seems to care.

Oh it's going to be a party, all right.

Judd clears his throat. "What I mean to say is, and forgive me for being blunt," he says in that attorney general voice of his that I'll bet scares most people. "Who are you to Sam?"

And there it is.

"That's easy," I say, putting on my sunglasses. "I'm the girl he tells all his secrets."

For the record, I don't hate weddings. They just make me sad because they remind me I'll never get the chance to have my own.

It's right around midnight when the booze runs out. There's always that scary window at a party when folks are drunk enough to pick fights but not drunk enough to do everyone else a favor and just pass out. I've sat through enough wedding receptions to know they turn into a wake the minute something runs out: wine, food, sober guys to dance with, toilet paper in the women's bathroom. Maybe that's why the bride and groom always leave early. One minute there's this sea of hopeful faces dancing to Justin Timberlake, and the next minute the place seems darker and the people left are yawning and seem a lot less interesting. Suddenly there are empty tables piled with dirty dishes and the DJ is playing *Every Rose Has Its Thorn.*

With the cops still parked down the road, Judd's made it clear that no one drives anywhere tonight; we're a good twenty miles from town, and besides, even the gas stations are closed by now. For once I agree with him. I overhear one guy say he's going to swim over to Canada for some wine—and he's serious. He's in the water all the way up to his chin before Johnny Thunder jumps in and drags him back to shore. I've only had a few sips of wine tonight and my head feels clear—which may or may not be the best way to tell Sam what I want to tell him. I'm sitting on a log bench by the bonfire, looking up at the night sky. I feel a hand on my shoulder and I think it's Sam, but when I turn around I'm face to face with Roxy.

Her breath hits my face like a sour fog. White lightning, all right.

"Where's Sam?" she says, leaning on me for balance. The words come out slurred like an old, warped cassette tape. "Where's my son?"

"I think he might be down by the lighthouse." I pat the bench next to me. "Why don't you sit with me for a while?"

"I need to talk to Sam," she says, pushing herself away. She takes a few ragged steps but stops, arms flailing to keep her balance. For a second it looks like she's going to drift right into the fire, so I jump up and grab the back of her shirt. At the last moment she changes direction, sailing out across the trampled grass towards the water. Then she stops again and peers up at the clear night sky. "This is bullshit, you *hear* me?" It takes me a moment to realize she's yelling at the stars. "Total bullshit."

Sam appears out of the dark and puts his hands around her shoulders to steady her. The two of them stand there for a minute, not moving, two dance partners tired of going over the same old steps. Judd and Johnny Thunder show up a few minutes later, along with a couple of the other New Dudes-in-Waiting in tow.

Roxy pounds her fist on Sam's chest a couple times. "You're avoiding me," she says. She's crying now. "I'm your mother, and you're avoiding me."

"What do you *want*?" Sam says, looking at the ground. "What do you want from me?"

She waits until he lifts his head so they're looking into each other's eyes. This is *Sam*—she could ask for anything right now, make any demand of her only son. But after a while she just looks away, spits into the dirt. "I want *wine*," she says. "I want you to give me some more wine."

"Roxy, you're drunk," I say, coming close enough to touch her back softly. "Maybe you've had enough."

"Oh, I'm drunk all right, little girl," she says, shrugging off my hand and slipping away from Sam, like she was stepping out of a dress. "But I'll never have enough."

"We're all out of wine anyway," Johnny Thunder says, trying to be helpful. He holds up an empty milk jug in his hand and turns it upside down, shaking it. "Like, seriously."

Judd comes up behind Sam and whispers into his ear; I can't catch it all but the last thing he says is, "Maybe it's time."

Sam sighs. "Johnny," he says with a raspy voice, sounding like he's out of breath. "Go over and dip your jug in the water." Johnny Thunder hears him but the big man stands there, bewildered. Sam points to the lake. "Just go ahead and do it."

Judd looks around; there's only the six of us standing here. "Go ahead," he says.

Johnny does what he's told. He walks over to the edge of the lake and bends down to dunk his jug into the water until it's mostly full.

Sam hasn't moved. "Take a sip," he says behind his back. "Trust me."

Johnny smells it first, then holds the jug up and takes a swig. "It's *good*," he says, taking another drink. "It's *damn* good."

"Make sure everyone gets some," he says, turning and walking away. "Especially my mother." He disappears into the darkness, and I follow him.

"Sam," I say, struggling to keep up with his long strides. "Some of those guys aren't going to understand. They don't know what they just saw."

"They saw me lose my temper," he says, letting me catch up. "I do it a lot."

We walk for about a half-mile along the water until Sam finally loses steam and slows down a little. We're into the woods now, and behind us we can barely hear the party in the distance. Sam finds a big rock and we sit down. He takes off his sandals and dangles his toes in the water. My legs are too short but I dangle anyway. We watch the little waves slap at the rough rocks along the shore. There's a ship passing by out there, and its lights move in the darkness like ghosts.

I hear Judd's voice in the darkness, getting closer. He's calling out for Sam.

"For the record, I don't trust that guy," I say.

"Judd's all right once you get to know him," Sam says. "He's really good with logistics, numbers, stuff like that. You know how bad I am at being organized."

I figure I've got two more minutes before Judd finds us and sucks Sam back to the party. So I do what I've wanted to do all day: I reach over and hold him, really hold him, leaning my head against his shoulder. His short beard feels like Brillo on my face, but I don't care. We sit there together, and I pretend we're a boy and a girl again.

"Come on," he says, kicking off his shoes and slipping off his shirt. Then he launches himself off the rock and plunges into the shallow water. He's standing in the chest-high water, hands out.

"But I'll ruin my dress," I say, and we both laugh.

He steadies himself on the rocks and reaches for my hand. "Trust me."

I slip off my shoes and slide down the rock to touch my big toe in the water. "God, it's cold," I say, turning it in a circle. "It's *fucking fucking fucking* cold."

He comes back to me, taking my arm and pulling me in; suddenly I'm up to my chin. I lose my balance on the rocky bottom and when I go under, I forget to close my mouth. In an instant my throat is full of water. I panic, and when I break the surface I'm thrashing my arms. But the water tastes sweet. We whip our wet clothes towards shore and then swim out a little deeper. We take turns splashing each other. It's weird, but now my skin doesn't feel all that cold. Honestly, I feel *warm*. Sam goes out even farther and raises his hand, beckoning for me to follow. I swim out to him and grab onto his shoulders when I get there. He holds my waist as we both tread water, and for that moment it feels like we're back in high school, night-swimming out at Rodriguez Lake.

I can hear Judd's voice getting louder.

Sam sighs and squeezes my hand. "I'll be back," he says, turning to shore.

"You're not coming back," I say. "You're going to be surrounded by dudes all night."

"We'll be alone again," he says. "Soon." But the somber droop in his voice reminds us that we won't, at least not in this life. When Sam climbs out of the water, there's this glint of moonlight on his wet skin that shows all the muscles in his back. I watch him fumble around in the tall grass, looking for his clothes; I remember that watching Sam put his clothes on has always been just as sexy as watching him take them off. When he slips his T-shirt over his head, he turns to wave at me. I wave back but when I do he's already disappearing down the path, back towards the lighthouse.

I paddle closer to shore until my feet find the uneven rocks at the bottom. When the water is down to my waist again I start to shiver; somehow the air feels colder than the water now, and I quickly fall back into the lake and tread water some more. I can see the smoldering light of the bonfire in the distance but I can't hear the voices around it anymore; the jamboree must finally be dying down. Some of the truck dogs are barking out a lonely chorus, restless from being chained up so late. I know I should get out soon and make sure Roxy doesn't drink herself to death, or make sure Laz hasn't joined a gang of biker-assassins—but right now this water feels so good, I don't want to.

Besides, I think I've forgotten where I threw my clothes.

In the darkness, I lie back flat and let my body float. I know they call this Lake Superior, but it sure feels like the ocean. When I spread out my arms and legs and draw deep breath, my belly button pokes above the water like a desert island. I take another deep gulp of air and let the current take my body. I know I should be more frightened, being out here alone, but for now I don't mind the solitude. With the waves gently lapping at my ears, the only sound I hear is this strange monotone that hums like bumblebees.

All hail the Queen Bee of Want, floating alone again.

When I wake up tomorrow, I know things will be the same: I'll still be sleeping in a car five hundred miles from home. I'll still want the same exact things I want today. I'll still stew over not being able to write my own story the way I want it. It's a little scary, this sudden feeling of weightlessness, but it makes me remember something Roxy told me years ago, the Roxy I want to remember, when I was a girl: sometimes you've got to let life make the choices. Sometimes you've got to let the story write you.

I let myself sail further away from shore. I feel something nip at my heel but right now I'm too comfortable to move, and for the moment I forget about the million or so critters that must be swimming and crawling around me in the blackness. When the water starts to feel a little colder on my skin, I know I'm drifting out even deeper. For the moment, I forget my feet can't touch the bottom.

First Epistle of Paul to the Romans

Summer 2011

To: Poncho S. Pelotti, Acting Commissioner <ppelotti@ irs.gov>

From: Patrick Sullivan, Special Agent IRS-CI <psulliva3@ irs.gov>

cc: <ksanford@irs.gov>

Re: Re: Re: Progress Report?

Hi Punchy:

You really want a progress report? Okay here it is:
AMERICA IS IN A WORLD OF SHIT.

This thing has Waco written all over it. Like Yogi said, *déjà vu all over again*, my friend: there's even one group up here with their very own compound (a whole island this time! whoa!) and a "spiritual leader" who kind of looks like David Koresh, minus the goofy glasses. Ring a bell, Punch? The more time I spend up here, the more I'm convinced we should just dig a big hole, throw in all these militia groups, gun nuts, survivalists and all the other assorted wackjobs we got living in the woods, bulldoze it all over and cover it with a mini-mall. You want my opinion? The only thing more dangerous to America than these camouflaged hicks running around the woods with their AK-47s and hunting knives are the ones who say they're doing it because they're on a mission from God.

We got real trouble up here, and I'm getting too old to hide in the bushes and tail these nutjobs around in their pickup trucks, waiting for them to jaywalk or steal some other hill-billy's cow so we can make an arrest.

Patriot Act, my ass. Since when did the Midwest start feeling like the Middle East?

Btw Punch thanks so much for putting me in charge of this "important task force" (I pasted that straight from your last e-mail.) You asshole.

Remember me, your old friend Sully? The guy two years ahead of you at Cornell? The guy who gave you your nickname after you knocked out those two townies at Pulaski's? The guy who got you laid by Mandy Castellano at the Enchantment Under the Sea Dance junior year? The guy who also held your hand at the doctor's when it turned out she had crabs?

There comes a point in a man's life when there's too much mileage on the odometer.

Don't get me wrong: you know I love my job. If I wasn't working the field for IRS I'd have to find another way to track down embezzlers or catch some fatcat in a lie. After all, we're the ones who got Capone, we solved the Lindbergh kidnapping, and we even cleaned up baseball. Remember the good old days, when criminals robbed banks or jewelry stores and did the sensible thing, like buy sportscars or retire to Costa Rica? These militia groups are different. They don't act like normal crooks. They walk around with these dumb smiles on their faces and they say "Praise the Lord" when you walk by. (No, I'm serious!) They're like zombies, or cockroaches. Or maybe zombie cockroaches.

Take this one gang we're tracking now: they call themselves the SICARII, and I don't need the nerds at Langley or Quantico to tell me that's Latin or Swahili or something for "Bunch of Dirty Stinking Cutthroat Assholes." Two or three years ago they were just another bike cult: prostitution, booze, car parts, running drugs down from Canada, all the usual recreational sports. Now enter this granola hippie from North Dakota named Sam Davidson, and suddenly it's all Peace and Love. You got people coming from all over to hear this guy talk about puppy dogs and ice cream, and the whole time these Sicarii guys are business as usual: their latest bright idea is to smuggle their blow by sending fishing boats across Lake Superior. (Btw my contacts at Langley say they've managed to get someone on the inside of the group, but I'm not holding my breath. They told us the same thing at Waco, and we both know what happened to *that* guy.)

Like I said, the brainwashed zombies on some kind of special mission from God are the one's you've got to look out for.

Hopefully we'll find something on a wacko like this Sam Davidson and give him the same treatment we gave Tim McVeigh: a nice speedy trial, a nice last meal, and then a nice lethal injection. End of story.

How does it happen? The zombies, I mean. One day you're working at the gas station or the Home Depot, minding your own business and saving up for the kids' college fund, and the next day you decide to throw your whole life away and follow some average Joe or back alley Sally around the country because you're convinced he must be the Messiah. I've never understood it, Punch – is there a sudden flash of lightning, an explosion? Does an angel appear in the living room and tell them what to do? I guess the answer is above my pay-grade.

I guess it's like my new friend up here, Matty Ice says: if God keeps on making roaches, we'll keep on stomping them out.

Okay, that's all for now. I got to get back to my important work, squatting in the bushes.

Give my best to Gia and the girls. You asshole.

Big Hugs & Kisses,
Sully

(sent from my iPhone)

Parable of the Prodigal Son

Winter 1998

Y ou can hear the hooker in the next room faking an orgasm. You know she's faking because she's narrating *everything*; you know she's a hooker because you heard the same story last night. *Now I'm riding you, baby, oh yeah you see how I'm riding you?* You're stuck in the same story, too: alone in Bismarck again, sitting on a motel toilet with a shotgun in your lap, but you can't pull the trigger. Your legs are starting to go numb from sitting on the can so long. At least this time your gun is loaded; the first time you decided to kill yourself, you forgot to buy the shells.

You laugh because that's your whole life: a gun without bullets.

You could die a happy man if one person in this whole wicked world remembered your name. At the Walmart, you bought the twenty gauge under the name Dwight D. Eisenhower, half-hoping you'd be caught in a background check, but the guy at the counter didn't blink an eye. Even your parole officer just points at you and calls you "guy" when you walk in his office. You're a man forgotten by the rest of the world. You are faceless even in your own dreams. When your mother was dying last year you went to the hospital to see her; she turned to the nurse and asked who you were. She looked right through you like a ghost. You blame the Alzheimer's, but she kept calling all the nurses by name: Rita, Corey and this hockey puck of a woman everyone called Little Flo. Sometimes you even forget your own name.

It's Dill Pembo, but no one really cares.

Back in high school, your English class spent weeks on *Old Man and the Sea*, but only thing you remember was Mr. Deegan saying the guy who wrote it did himself in like this: sitting with a shotgun. That sounded romantic at the time, but here you are alone in a cheap motel room with the scent of ammonia and old piss that reminds you of your old GP cell back at James River. The bars on the windows, the concrete balcony outside and the heavy chain on the alarm clock don't help either. When you did your first stretch—eighteen months for receiving—they put you in with some old coot who wouldn't stop talking about killing himself. What was his name? You can't remember. He talked with a cowboy accent like he was from Alabama or Utah or something. Every morning when you rolled out for head count he'd stand next to you and announce some new crazy way to commit suicide, yelling like an auctioneer. Tuesday it might be "Drinking a gallon of Lighter Fluid through your nose!" and Wednesday was "Jumping into a jet engine right before takeoff!" You got fed up with him quick, but some other dude in the block got fed up even quicker, because he strangled the old man to death right in the middle of TV time. You don't remember that dude's name, either, but you know for sure the television had *The Love Boat Movie* on.

Mr. Deegan would've called that irony.

You don't remember all that much from high school—too much malt liquor, too many distractions—but after old Deegan made the class read something, he'd always give the same goofy bullshit speech about how *every life is like a book*. He'd always write the same question on the chalkboard—*What kind of book do you want your life to be?*—and make you spend the last few minutes of class writing an answer in your composition book. Usually you didn't write anything, and when you did it was fantasies about driving hotrods like Richard Petty or banging chicks on the beach like Elvis. You would waste the time writing your name over and over again in the margins until it looked strange: Dill Pembo. Your mother named you after a weed. Back then it was your best attempt at a pickup line. *Hey pretty lady, I'm Dill—yeah, like the weed, so even if you say No, I'm still coming back.* You got a lot of beers in the face, but it did work once.

Her name was Roxy Boone.

She tossed beer in your face, too, but she did end up marrying you.

Now you are forty-eight. If you had to answer the old teacher's question now, you'd confess you are the kind of book people try to give away at yard sales, a buck for the whole box. You're the frayed and yellow paperback with the cover ripped off, the kind that's been kept in the cellar so long it smells like mud.

You are the book with the good parts already ripped out.

Mr. Deegan probably would've called that a metaphor.

You still think about her. It's been so long, but you really have no one else to think about. Roxy Boone, the only person who said she loved you out loud. It was probably a tired lie, but it's what you've got. That lie got you through a few years in prison. Like everything else in this world, though, it faded away to an echo. You had a life together. You shared a rented house back in Nazareth, but you haven't been anywhere near that town since she left you that night at the motel. She used to always say, *I'm a girl who knows her way around a motel* but the truth is she was only there because of you. Whenever you tell this story, you want to buy a shotgun.

Whenever you tell this story, you leave out a lot of details.

Once upon a time you shot a man in a North Dakota motel. It's really the only story you have worth telling; sometimes you tell it to whatever poor slob is sitting next to you at the bar. A lot of times you end up just telling it to yourself. You try to convince yourself all that time with Roxy was a story worth telling, too—a real love story—but deep down you know that's a lie; she never really loved you, and if you're honest, you were never a man worth loving.

The story starts at this old motel that used to sit right there on the interstate, right above Exit 261; the name escapes you but it had these rooms with movie themes. You remember it was the dead of winter and you remember the pool, too, of course. You would have gone back there today to shoot yourself—call it *closure*—but they tore that place down years ago. Now they've got a Dan's and a do-it-yourself car wash in the same spot.

Who are you kidding: you don't deserve your own story. When you die, no one is going to sit around the campfire and mystify small children with the Tales of Dill. No one is going to sing your ballad in a smoky bar. The best you can hope for is to be remembered by someone else. You're not a chapter, you're not even a paragraph; the best you can do is a footnote.

That's not much, but it's what you've got.

Only one person has ever cared enough about you to remember you. You heard she's back in Nazareth now, living with a new man and bringing up that same abandoned kid, Sam. It's been almost seventeen years, and she probably still hates your guts. Maybe she always will.

You don't want anything from her; this is not about winning someone back. You realize your days of winning anything are long gone. The bar is low: all you want is someone to see that you exist. You don't even care if those eyes are filled with love or hate. You just want another human being to acknowledge you're alive. At this point in your life, you'd rather be hated than forgotten.

You would take the hate. After all, to hate someone you have to remember them.

You step off the bus in a Kum n' Go parking lot on the edge of Route 85 and you wonder if this is going to be either the bravest or the dumbest thing you've ever done. Last time you were in Nazareth, it was barely after New Year's in 1983 and you were in the van, headed the other way, back towards Bismarck. On the ride up here today you expected to barely recognize the place, but it's all coming back to you now: the tractor graveyard is still there outside Annie's shop, but it's all choked with tall weeds. Nazareth doesn't look a whole lot different than what you remember. This gas station used to be a Gas n' Sip, but it's still a gas station. Down the way you can see the same old Red Rooster, and beyond that the dusty fairgrounds. The burnt musk of barley and durum wheat brings you back. You look south towards the Badlands and a rush of faded memories pass through your mind. You mumble, "Welcome home Dill Pembo" but it doesn't sound right; *home* is the wrong word, even though this is the closest you'll ever come to a home-coming.

Welcome Home Dill Pembo, you old bastard, you dirty son of a bitch.

It's a half-mile walk from the highway into town, and when you start down the road you see something else that jars your memory: a Galilee County sheriff's cruiser, parked alongside the road about fifty yards ahead of you. Instantly a jagged streak of lightning runs down your back—you think of Severo Rodriguez, and the old memory freezes every muscle in your neck and jaw. You know he's been dead for years, but that doesn't make anything softer. You remember the Old Bear sitting in his pickup truck in almost the exact same spot, waiting to see if anyone new got off the bus. Even now you can smell his cigar smoke wafting out from the cracked window.

You pass the cruiser and you see a fat guy sitting there in the same rust-brown uniform you remember, looking at you through a pair of gold-rimmed sunglasses. He's too young to be Severo, though. He rolls down the window. "Welcome to Nazareth, stranger. Can we help you find something?" You can't get a good look at his face as you pass by, but something in his voice sure sounds familiar.

You keep walking. "Just visiting an old friend."

The door opens and he gets out. "What's your name?" he says, spitting into the asphalt before standing up and rearranging his belt. "We like to keep tabs on new folks."

You stop, turning to face him. "It's Dill Pembo. I used to live here, a long time ago."

He mouths your name a couple times, then shakes his head. "Don't ring a bell," he says. "You lived in Nazareth a long time, you say?"

"All my life. Well, minus the last seventeen." As you come a little closer, you're certain you've seen him before. "Hey, are you Phil Rodriguez?"

"Felipe was my brother," he says, folding his arms. "He died some time back."

"I'm sorry to hear that," you say. "You must be little Anton, then. Folks called you—"

"I know what folks *called* me," Anton snaps. He paces a little back and forth next to the car. "Dill Pembo. Yeah, now it's coming back. Roxy Boone's old squeeze. Last we heard, you were down in Williston—what was it? Shearing sheep? Plucking chickens?"

"Hogs," you say, looking down. "I had a job feeding hogs. That was years ago." It was the last full-time work you had, and it was the worst job you could ever imagine, worse than prison.

"Yeah that's it—hogs. You know how slow news travels out here." He sure sounds amused now. "Hog feeding, now there's a career move if I ever heard one. So, what brings you back to Nazareth?"

"Thought I'd pay Roxy a visit. Been a long time."

He laughs out loud. "She know you're coming?"

"Not exactly," you say, shrugging your shoulders. "I'm kind of playing it by ear."

"Should be one hell of a visit, then," he says, letting out a long whistle. "But I guess every hog has his day."

"I'm not here to start any trouble," you say, jerking your thumb back towards the highway. "You saw I just stepped off the bus from Bismarck."

He stares at you for a long time. "Well, the bus back comes at quarter-to-eight," he says, getting back into the car and slamming the door. "Make sure you're on it."

You have to go through town to get to Roxy's house. Along the way you see a lot more memories: Andy's Place looks exactly the same as you left it, down to the crack in the dirty window out front. You half-expect to go in there and find your beer on the back table, still sweating. The people you pass on the street don't give you a second look, though. Part of you wants to yell out, "It's me! Dill! I'm back!" but you know no one would care.

The house is a big place on the north end of town, her mom's old house; three floors with a wraparound porch and a long dirt driveway. You don't see any cars but there's a girl sitting on the front stoop, her arms folded. Did Roxy have a daughter, too? She doesn't look like Roxy but she's still pretty, in a Joan Jett kind of way. "Does Roxy Boone live here?"

"You from Bismarck?"

You're a little surprised. "Yes, yes I am—how did you know that?"

Her eyes light up a little. She stands up. "So you've got news about Sam?"

You're about to ask this girl what the hell's going on when you hear a diesel engine grumble behind you. You turn around to see a big pickup truck lumbering slowly up the drive. Before it comes to a stop, the girl on the porch has already slipped past you; she runs to the passenger door, peering in the window. You recognize Roxy right away sitting in the passenger seat, but from the puzzled expression on her face, it's clear she has no idea who you are.

Your stomach twists. Yeah, definitely the dumbest thing you've ever done.

The big guy driving must be her husband: when he steps out of the truck, you notice how big he really is. You heard she had a husband, but you didn't know he was the size of a grain elevator. He looks at you with suspicion. There's a teenage boy in the back seat, too, but he's too busy getting a hug from the porch girl to notice you.

"Hey Roxy," you say, offering a weak wave. "It's me, Dill."

She gets out and slams the door shut: she recognizes you all right. Without a word she motors past you up the steps and rips open the screen door to the house. You can hear her yelling up a storm in there. You blurt out the first thing that comes into your head: "I almost killed myself last night."

She opens the screen door and stomps back out onto the porch. "Keep standing in front of that truck and I'll finish the job for you."

"I'm serious," you say. She disappears into the house again. "I had a gun to my head." You tap two fingers against your ear as if to demonstrate. That's when you feel a hand on your shoulder; you've forgotten the giant husband has been standing behind you the whole time. You expect him to beat you to a pulp, but he doesn't. Not yet, anyway. He turns you around, then rubs the stubble on his chin. He's sizing you up. "I think she's a little surprised."

"Listen, I know this is awkward. I don't want money, and I don't want to sell you anything. I'm not here on some crazy quest to get her back, or spill some long-lost secret, either."

"This is fucking weird."

"I know. I just want a chance to talk to her, to say some things."

What happens next might be the definition of *awkward silence.*

"Let me talk to her," he finally says to you with a sigh. "If she doesn't come out, least I can do is give you a ride back to the highway. But I'm telling you right now," he says, coming closer until he blocks out the sun. "If you make her cry, I'm dragging you back to the highway behind the truck."

"Deal," you say.

The teenage boy is out of the truck now. "You're Dill," the kid says.

You nod. "And I'm guessing you're Sam," you say. "We met once, a long time ago."

"I know," the kid says. "You're the guy who went blind from the pool."

"You remember that?"

"My mom's a pretty good storyteller," he says.

Roxy cracks the screen door open. "So what did you do, find God or something?"

You turn to her and just shake your head. "No, nothing like that."

You figure you could find God, no problem. God would probably have more trouble finding you.

She folds her arms across her chest. "Did you really have a gun to your head?"

"It was in my lap," you say. "But I'm pretty sure it was loaded. Anyway, I couldn't do it."

She smiles. "You were always shitty at following through. Dill, why are you here? I mean, why now?"

"This is going to sound stupid," you say. "But I guess I just needed someone to remember who I was."

"Of course I'm going to remember you," she says. "Bad times are still times."

You must be smiling a lot, because she says, "What are you smiling about?"

"Honestly, I didn't think I'd get a chance to sit here and talk to you. I came up here expecting the worst."

"You almost got it," she says. "Joe kind of talked me off a ledge in there."

"What did he say to make you come out here?"

"He reminded me that in a crazy way, you kind of saved my life."

"*Ruined* your life, you mean."

"Back then it sure felt like you ruined it," she says. "But if you didn't do what you did, I never would have had Sam," she says. "And I would never have met Joe. I can't imagine my life now without either of them."

"Joe's a good man."

"I know," she says. "We just got back from Bismarck ourselves. Sam kind of got himself lost on a class trip yesterday, so we had to go get him."

"He seems like a sharp kid."

She looks up at the darkening sky. "Trust me, you have no idea."

You sit and talk about old times for a while. It's easier than you imagined, awakening some old ghosts. It feels good to finally talk to her. Once in a while you can hear Joe coming to the door, listening for thunder and lightning.

"Well, an hour ago I couldn't imagine saying this, but," she says, drawing a deep breath, "It's actually good to see you, Dill."

"It's really good to be seen," you say.

"That reminds me, how are your eyes?"

"Oh, fine," you say. "They only hurt when I swim."

In a few more minutes, you'll get up from this chair. You will hug Roxy like an old friend and then you will say good-bye. You know you'll never see her again, but you feel happier than you have in a long time. You have no idea where you're headed next; you're still homeless, which is really the same thing as being nameless. But at least now you know your name is written down somewhere. This might only be a metaphor, but as you walk slowly back towards the highway, you can feel a page or two being added to your book.

The Transfiguration

Autumn 2011

Pete was ready to believe in miracles. June hadn't left their bed since Tuesday, but he was the one sick of everything: sick of the pills and drips and ointments with names he couldn't pronounce, sick of the sympathetic phone calls and e-mails that always ended with *Thinking of You*, tired of the stupid pamphlets people left behind with titles like *Curing Cancer With Classical Music* and *The Vegan Cancer Diet*. They were both barely forty years old but the house looked like it belonged to a couple twice their age, a cluttered graveyard of useless things: empty medicine bottles, collapsible walkers and ergonomic canes, a fold-up wheelchair, green oxygen tanks, get well cards, shiny balloons, stuffed bears, stuffed bunny rabbits, stuffed birds, a stuffed octopus that said, *"I've got plenty of arms to hold you!"* when you pressed the right tentacle, scented candles, gift baskets, plastic vases full of roses or daisies or fruit, anonymous casseroles and bundt cakes. *Oh God*, Pete thought, *the fucking casseroles.* Since the dawn of time, this is how the middle-aged women of Wisconsin fought cancer: they dumped shit-ty macaroni and cheese in an aluminum tub and left it on your kitchen table when you weren't looking.

The worst part was realizing he was just as useless. Some days he would call his brother and say he was sick, too, only to spend the day driving around the county in their empty cargo van, making pretend deliveries. He'd sit on the side of the road for hours, thinking about the best way to kill him-self if June went; suicide seemed a lot less scary than living the rest of his life without her. He wasn't a coward. He would do just about anything if it meant making her well again: rob a bank, derail a train, poison a well. He didn't care. He'd murder a stranger to save her; hell, in the heat of the moment, he would probably kill a friend.

In the end, he was that rare and dangerous thing: a man in love with his wife.

Pete pulled off his rubber boots on the porch before opening the screen door and stepping inside, padding softly across the linoleum in his thick wool socks. This late in the season, he'd get back from the docks around seven in the morning, but today he was a couple hours early on account of last night's run being so lousy. Their daughter Stacey was asleep on the living room sofa, remote dangling from her hand. There was no sound from the TV but he could see an infomercial playing, one he'd seen plenty of times during his own sleepless nights: some guy in a cheesy polyester sweater and moustache droning on about how drinking fresh juice can cure just about anything. He felt like laughing, but he didn't want to wake anyone and besides, he ordered the damned machine himself about a month ago. It was somewhere out on the porch, still in the UPS box, stacked like Mayan ruins with all the other objects of late-night desperation he'd purchased since June had got the bad news. There was an air purifier that also played soothing whale songs, a do-it-yourself detox kit that said it sucked the poisons out of your body with candles and space-age suction cups, a set of wrist and ankle magnets that are guaranteed to cure any disease by redirecting your electrical energy flow. A whole room full of miracles.

Turns out the world was full of miracles. They even came with free shipping.

Stacey stirred behind him, brushing her face with the back of her hand as she rolled over on the cramped couch. She was a good kid, and she was good with her mom. Standing there in the doorway, Pete felt guilty about not paying more attention to their daughter; he couldn't remember much about being nineteen, but he knew it must have sucked. For a moment he thought about waking Stacey up and asking her the standard dad-type questions: if she planned on giving college another try, or if she was seeing anyone new. But he didn't feel up to it, and besides, Stacey was a smart girl; she'd notice he was out of his depth right away. June had always been the one she'd go to with any real problems.

Pete stepped carefully through the living room and down the back hallway to the master bedroom. After twenty years, he'd done enough repairs on this old house to know which floorboards were going to creak, even in the dark. He peered through the open door to the bedroom, listening for her breathing. He expected her to be asleep at this hour, but her eyes were fluttering open. "You're up?" he said, stepping closer.

"I think so," she groaned slowly. "Hard to tell with the morphine."

"How are you feeling?" Pete said, sitting on the edge of the bed. He knew it was a stupid question; a few months ago this same woman would run five or six miles every morning. She even talked about the Duluth marathon.

"Same as yesterday," she said, managing a little smile. "Like I been hit by a train."

"There's other things we can try," he said, bending down and smoothing a fold of her blanket. "The chemo might not have worked, but I've got some promising leads." That was a bald lie, just like the hopeful, cheery note in his voice was a lie, but right now telling lies felt easier than telling the truth.

She rubbed her forehead. "Tell me you haven't been on the internet again."

"So what if I have," he said, turning away. "We've got nothing to lose."

June shook her head. "Last time you went on there, you found a witch doctor in Hong Kong who pulls your organs out, waves a stick over them, and shoves them back in."

"It was the Philippines," he said. "And anything's worth a look."

"No it *ain't*," she said, letting out a tired sigh. "Sooner or later, everyone in this world runs out of chances."

"Don't say that," he said, standing up. "Don't ever say that to me again."

"Oh, honey," she said, slowly lifting her hand to brush the back of his leg. "What in the world are you going to do when I'm gone?"

He kept his face turned, pretending to look at the pictures they had on top of the dresser across the room. He didn't want June to see his eyes tearing up. The pictures always made it worse: everyone in them was smiling, not a care in the world. He felt sick to his stomach.

"I'll tell you what you're going to do," she continued, breathing a little harder. "First, you donate the five tons of mac and cheese out there to the sailor's shelter," she said, pointing towards the kitchen. "Well, all except the ones my sister made. They probably wouldn't accept those."

"Probably make perfect anchors for the boats," Pete said, rubbing his soggy eyes.

She turned to glance at the digital clock on the nightstand. "Speaking of which, don't you have fish to catch this morning, skipper?"

"We're going out tonight," he said, wiping his eyes. "Summer's winding down, so Andy wants to try for cisco."

June let out a moan. "I miss night-fishing with you guys. I miss having folks over and frying up a big batch of fish, too."

She rolled over on her side until the tube in her arm pulled her back. "God, I miss food altogether."

He cranked his mouth open, manufacturing a smile. "Are you kidding? We're having Thanksgiving at our house this year. Just like old times: turkey, roast potatoes, all the kids at the kiddie table—cousin Ernie showing up with another hooker, everything."

"Oh yeah? And who's cooking this feast?"

"You are," he said, bending down to kiss her forehead. "You are."

He thought about sharing the story he'd heard on the pier that morning, but she started to drift off again. *Maybe it's for the best*, he thought; she'd probably just laugh at him some more when he told her what Andy had told him about Sheriff Long's boy. Another miracle to add to the pile on the porch. No need to get her excited this early.

He stroked her matted hair, listening to her breathe.

I am not a coward, he mumbled under his breath. Pete sat there for a while, wondering how far he would go to save her. What would he do to bring her back to him? "Anything," he instantly muttered to himself. It was a reflex like any other. Whether he believed it or not, that was something different.

I am not a coward.

When he was a boy, he used to think his mother was crazy for slapping him across the chest whenever the car stopped suddenly, as if that would save him from death, a mother's antidote to simple inertia and physics. But now he could see that was merely her reflex, a split-second reaction by a mother who would do anything, even defy gravity, to save a child from death. When his youngest brother Charlie drowned fifteen years back, she'd never been the same since. She didn't drive much anymore, but once Pete saw her back the car out of the driveway and slap the empty seat beside her when she saw someone walking behind her on the sidewalk; she was still hoping to save someone, anyone, still haunted by that old reflex.

He heard Stacey stirring in the other room. In a minute, she would come in and beg him to go lie down and finally get some sleep, but he didn't want sleep. Every day was a drowsy blur anyway. Pete sat motionless, staring out the window at the grey morning. He was so tired he couldn't tell if the dead weight that had settled in his gut for so long was desperation or hope. These days he didn't see any difference between the two. *Maybe despair is when you know better*, he thought. But right now he didn't care. Right now he was hoping the fish story they told him last night was true. He hoped for a chance to talk to this Sam Davidson, face to face.

He was hoping for a miracle.

This was a bad idea. Tom sat in the deserted marina parking lot, sipping black coffee from a Styrofoam cup. Every so often he'd run the heater in the car so the windows would stop fogging up. He was half hoping this Lazlo guy didn't show at all. If there was a history of bad ideas, he thought, this one had to rank near the top—maybe even the Abraham Lincoln of bad ideas, or at least the Ronald Reagan. But Judd was the one giving the orders, and he seemed to know what he was doing so far. Tom didn't like the whole setup, but he was here anyway, ready to take a few chances; there was a chance this little operation could finally get him out of here, once and for all. Four days of grunt work out on the water seemed like a small price to pay for a new life.

Besides, his Glock 40 was stowed in his duffel if the price suddenly got higher.

Tom Lowey was only twenty-six, but he'd already had his own long history of bad ideas, a lengthy list of escape attempts from his own boring world on the rez at Bad River. By the time he finished tribal school he'd already joined a band, trained for his Wisconsin CDL, even gone down to Ashland to enlist in the Marines—their doctor said his heart beat the wrong way. The last thing he wanted to do was spend his whole life here, repeating his father and older brother's lives like another bad sequel. Growing up on Bad River, the choices for a young Chippewa really didn't seem like choices at all: waiting tables at the casino like his sisters, working the backwoods for BLM like his brothers, maybe taking over a boat from his uncle Silas and smelling like fish the rest of his life.

A man can want a bigger life, Silas told him, even if he didn't know exactly what it was.

The coffee was only lukewarm now but Tom drank it anyway, the row of gill net tugs along the pier hypnotizing him as he watched them bob up and down, up and down through the windshield. Cape Ernum was a study in grey: the water, the sky, even the birds. Once in a while he stole a glance at the rearview mirror, wondering when this new guy would show. Two jaegers were back there now, taking turns stabbing their beaks into an old hamburger bun. When he caught his own reflection in the dim morning light he managed to smile at what he saw, cocking the blue Minnesota Twins ball cap on his head even further to one side. The frayed hat had been his brother's; just like everything else in his family, it was passed down after being squeezed of any real life. In fact, everything he had right now was borrowed: his parka, his rubber boots, the half-pack of GPCs tucked in his shirt pocket, this battered Honda Civic with no muffler and about a million miles on it. Even the dog sleeping in the backseat wasn't really his, but Tom figured no one would miss Dud around the house for a few days. Besides, he thought, a mutt that big and ugly might come in handy on a trip like this.

The part that worried him most was including Lazlo Hooker. The poor guy had no idea what he was getting himself into. Milk Dud woofed from the backseat and popped his head up.

"I see him, Dud." Tom watched the skinny dude in the rearview, coming down the empty street towards the docks. Tom opened the door and poured the last of his coffee out.

"You're late," he yelled, reaching down to pull the trunk release on the battered Civic. Then he clapped his hands and the dog came to life, bolting out onto the asphalt and shaking the sleep off his mottled brown coat.

Lazlo Hooker. This guy was dressed for a picnic or something, with white pants, docksiders and a striped shirt. He had a knapsack hanging off one shoulder, which Tom hoped was carrying the money.

Laz took one look at Dud and groaned. "Tell me we're not bringing the dog."

"This here's Milk Dud," Tom said, patting the dog's fat head. "He's a water dog, all right." He went around to the trunk and banged on it a few times until it popped open. Tom hoisted out the two buckets of herring and dropped them on the pavement.

When Laz peered in the trunk, he pinched his nose. "What the hell is that smell?"

"That's our bait," Tom said. "If we're going to act like we're fishing out there, professor, then we need bait." He saw the blank look on Laz's face. "Don't you know anything about fishing?"

"I've been to Red Lobster three or four times."

Tom closed his eyes and rubbed the bridge of his nose, feeling a four-day migraine coming on. This job was sounding worse all the time; all he needed was to be out on the deep water of Superior with someone who probably got seasick in the bathtub. "Well, if Judd speaks for you, I guess that's good enough for me." He slammed the trunk shut.

"Now help me stow this gear on the boat."

Together they made their way down the empty pier, Tom looking over his shoulder every so often; the last thing he needed was running into someone who knew him. He patted his jacket, double checking that the two-way radio Judd had given him was still in there.

Milk Dud had stopped to sniff at a dead bird halfway down the pier. "Dud," Tom barked. "Let's go, fella." The dog broke into a wobbly gallop to catch up.

The *Goosey Lucy* was a forty-five foot sport fisher that sat alone at the end of the pier. Silas wouldn't be missing it for the next couple days; the old man had been cooped up in the hospital down in Ashland, recovering from gallstone surgery. And from what Judd had told him, no one would miss this Lazlo Hooker character for a couple days, either. The weather report had promised clear skies, but Tom knew that didn't mean much; once you cleared the shoals off Oil Press Island and made deep water, you could find yourself inside a full-blown typhoon without any place to hide. But that was a chance he was willing to take.

When Nick saw the old army Jeep parked in front of the Captain Flint, he knew court was now in session. Around Cape Ernum, it was common knowledge Key Conway conducted most of his business in the back booth of the shanty bar. The judge had a big office in the new county courthouse down the street, but he rarely used it for anything more important than an afternoon nap. There was even a rumor around town that a couple summers ago he married an out-of-town couple right over the pinball machine. Nick knew the rumor was true; after all, he was one of the witnesses. He also knew there was a copy of the good book stuffed somewhere under the beer taps, just in case it happened again.

Nick Demuz hadn't taken a drink in thirty years, but whenever he was back in town from Madison, he found himself going in the Flint to talk with Key Conway. *Listen to Key might be a better description*, he thought; for such a skinny man, the judge sure could hold a lot of hot air. Nick missed the old days, before he got elected to the state Senate, when he could wake up mornings and walk down the steep hill from his house towards the docks and watch the water birds with absolutely nothing to do. One sunny morning he stood right here and saw a bull Moose swimming the mile or so across to Madeline Island, two herring gulls catching a slow ride on his fat antlers. Now folks called Nick at his house more than they called 9-1-1, and for stupid things: loud noises, bad smells, kids taking potshots at street signs with an airgun, random things going bump in the night. Such was the lot in life for a state senator. He always had an answer for them, but lately people had been calling up with stories a lot stranger. People kept calling him and talking about miracles—not the kind you see on YouTube these days, but real honest-to-God miracles, right in front of their eyes. For the first time in his life, Nick really had no idea what to believe.

He needed to talk with Key about this Sam Davidson.

The green Jeep tilted up on the curb, and with its two right tires riding high over the sidewalk it reminded Nick of a dog about to take a leak. The mangled front bumper leaned into one of the trees they'd planted last year for Earth Day, bending the little birch like a bow. As Nick walked past he checked its rusted belly for recent water damage; every once in a while the judge would forget to set the parking brake and the big car would roll down to the end of the dock, tipping into the harbor for a swim.

The sun was high but the wind made the day feel colder; a sharp wind was coming south off the islands, carrying the soft musk of aspen. Nick looked around the street before opening the screen door; he could do without some people seeing him go in a place like this; particularly, the people who voted. Inside the bar, Nick's eyes slowly adjusted to the dim. The place smelled liked smoked fish and rust. The only sunlight peeked through three or four little portholes up front. It was barely noon on a Tuesday so he expected the place to be empty except for Key and Veronica behind the bar, but when he stepped in he noticed those giant brothers who worked for Romack Fish at the front table, hunched over a couple bottles of Huber and whispering in low tones to one another. Veronica looked up to give him a sleepy nod as she wiped a spot on the bar with a towel.

"Hey Ronnie," Nick said to her, running his palm lightly along the splintered old wood of the bar. He could hear

Key growling at someone in the back. "Sounds like court's already in session."

"You could say that," she said, wiping her wet hands on her apron. She pulled a coffee mug off the drying rack and poured him some from the Bunn-O-Matic. "He's got Linus back there," she said, rolling her eyes.

Nick took a sip. "You know what about?" He had a good idea, but Veronica was the closest thing that Cape Ernum had to an information kiosk, so he asked anyway.

She smacked her gum, sneaking a quick glance at the two boys. "No clue, senator."

He took another sip of the coffee and picked up a few peanuts from the bowl and tossed them around in his hand like dice. "And I thought bartenders were good listeners."

"Not at all. We're a lot like you politicians," she said, leaning over the bar. "We're good at *pretending* to listen."

"You got me there," he said, smiling. He popped the peanuts into his mouth and turned to the two boys. "Hey, fellas," he said, patting the older one, Johnny, on the shoulder with his free hand. But the boy winced; Nick noticed too late that his arm was in a sling. "Oh gosh, sorry there, son. Not a work injury, I hope."

"We had a match down in Green Bay last week," Jimmy mumbled, staying hunched over the bar. He raised his bottle of beer. "Pete's got us doing a cisco run tonight, thought we might as well grab a burger and a few cold ones—but then the judge came in."

"Yeah, kind of lost our appetite after that," Johnny said, turning and looking towards the back. He turned back and both boys nodded to each other. They drained the last of their beers and pushed themselves up from the little table. "Thanks, Veronica."

"Catch a ton tonight, boys." She waved after them with her towel as they trudged outside. "Couple of good boys there," she said wistfully.

Nick nodded. "They sure seem sore about something, though."

Suddenly Key's voice burst from around the corner, filling the whole place. "Do I hear Nick? Is the Moose in the house? Ronnie, send his big Greek butt back here."

Nick shook his head and turned towards the back. *He knows I'm Albanian.*

"Nick the *Mooooooose*," Key said, his long, bony arms stretched out like he was guiding a plane to its gate. As far as Nick knew, the judge was the only one bent on calling him the Moose, probably because he used to have trouble pronouncing his family's name, *Demuz*. "Just in time, senator. Have a seat right here. I need a witness."

Nick saw that the judge was moving over in the bench to make room, but he sat down in the opposite booth anyway. Sheriff Long was sitting across from the judge; Nick had known Linus for years but he'd never seen his face like this, downcast like there was a death in the family. Nick knew the sheriff was a good man—former athlete, Iraq War vet—whose muscles stretched his shirt. Nick had already heard about Linus' oldest boy Trey, but he wanted to hear it first-hand, not from some anonymous gossip on a midnight phone call. "What do you need a witness for, judge?"

"I need someone else to hear this," Key growled, turning back to the sheriff. "Say it one more time. I dare you, Linus. Say that word once more and I swear I'll die right here and now."

Nick sipped his coffee. It looked like he would have to be diplomatic. "Say what word?"

"Miracle," the judge sneered. "You know what we have here, Moose? We got ourselves an *eyewitness*. That's right, first-hand testimony. And not just any testimony. Oh, no. We got it straight from a bonafide lawman, a *veteran*—who testifies we got a miracle worker on our hands."

"Sam Davidson," Nick added. "I've heard all the stories, too."

"Sam Davidson," Key repeated. "Sounds like a guy who sells insurance, not someone who raises the dead."

"I didn't say he raised the dead," Linus said. "I said he cured my boy."

Nick looked the sheriff up and down for clues. "Trey can walk now?"

Linus turned his head and looked Nick straight in the eye. "Sure as I'm sitting here talking to you, Nick. Come over for dinner if you want. Kid wants to try out for football next year. I'd have brought him over here to show you once and for all, but the boy hasn't stopped running since." He rubbed his nose. "Can't blame him, neither."

Key's adam's apple throbbed up and down like a broken thermometer. "You're missing quite a show up here, Moose. Two days ago I sent Deputy Dawg here to check this Davidson guy out—hell, maybe even get lucky and arrest him. But lo and behold, he comes back and says we got Helen-fucking-Keller walking around Jericho County."

Nick was still watching Linus; he noticed the sheriff's hands were shaking. The three men sat there for a while until Linus Long broke the silence. "You're a religious man, aren't you Nick?"

"You see his ass in the pew on the Sabbath, don't you?" Key laughed nervously. "Don't change the subject."

Nick held his hand up. "Hold on a minute, Key. Let the man talk." He folded his hands around his warm cup. "Well, to answer your question—yes, I guess I know scripture better than most."

Linus nodded and took a deep breath. "I've never been much for religion, you know? Never really believed in any of that stuff. Went to church mostly because my wife told me to. But now ... now, I don't know how to explain it. Couple nights ago I went to hear Sam talk, and it wasn't what I expected at all. Afterwards me and him got to talking, and it came up that my boy has the Lou Gehrig's and all. Next thing I know we're back at my house. Hour later, Trey walks down the stairs all by himself."

Nick wanted to be sure. "Anyone else there saw this?"

"Plenty. Go by the school right now if you don't believe me. He's playing kickball with the other kids."

Key scoffed. "Sounds like Grade A Brainwashing to me. That's what this guy does, he goes around telling stories and brainwashing people. Remember that Korean guy twenty years ago? It's all a trick. Don't get me wrong, I'm happy your kid can walk and all, but that doesn't make this stranger some kind of holy man."

Linus stood his ground. "You can't explain a miracle."

"There's that fucking word again. Now let me tell *you* something," Key said, picking up his cell phone from the carved table and dangling it in the air in front of Linus' head. "While you been out getting brainwashed by hippies I've been making calls, doing your fucking job. Talked to a guy out in North Dakota by the name of Rodriguez. He's the sheriff where this Sam Davidson comes from," he said. "Some desert hole-in-the-wall called Nazareth. Anyway, this Rodriguez fella says Davidson's a real troublemaker. Says he's got a record. Didn't say shit about miracles."

Nick scratched at his thick shock of salt-and-pepper hair. "I agree we've suddenly got a lot of strangers around, and some of them are pretty unsavory characters. But we just can't lump them all together. I think we should find out more about this Davidson fella."

"What you want to do, invite him for tea and cookies? No, sir. This is our town. He's turning it into a circus out there. I heard he drew five thousand out at Big Bay park last week, listening to every word he said. I think we should run him out of town now, let him do his miracles someplace else. If it were up to me, I'd hang the bastard.

Forty years ago when my daddy was judge around here, they probably would."

Nick let out a nervous laugh. "Okay, Key. Calm down. Last time I checked, Wisconsin doesn't have the death penalty."

"Thought about that," Key said, tapping his temple. His voice dwindled to a whisper, and he leaned closer to the table, his dark eyes darting around. "We get the Feds to prosecute him, then. Don't you know someone down at the U.S. Attorney's office in Madison?"

Nick stood up now, his eyes wide with amazement. "You're serious."

"Like smallpox. I'm surprised at you, Moose. You probably got the most to lose if we let these hooligans run wild around here. People don't re-elect their state senator when he can't keep the streets safe. And besides, you're the richest man on Lake Superior. Think about it."

Nick turned away without saying anything and headed for the door. He walked past Veronica without saying a word, his head bowed. Key had always been ambitious, he thought, but ambition without morality was a dangerous thing.

"This is the twenty-first century, Moose," Key called after him. "There's no such thing as miracles." Nick's eyes stung as he emerged into the bright sunlight. He still didn't know what to believe, but was sure of one thing now: time was running out.

From the wheelhouse, Pete noticed only a few herring gulls coming out to meet them as he made the slow turn around Hermit Island on the last leg home. *Great,* he thought; *even the birds know we had another shitty night.* Usually there would be hundreds of them dancing around the bow and dive-bombing the boats, hoping to steal a few loose fish before they made it into the warehouse. Nine hours trolling the deep water out past Sandy Island, and they only had a few hundred pounds in the hold to show for it. Andy trailed a few hundred yards behind in the *Murmillo*; from the gloom in his brother's voice on the radio, it didn't sound like they had done much better. One more summer like this and they'd have to quit. Maybe it was inevitable, Pete thought; you couldn't fish lake trout anymore, and any whitefish under seventeen inches you had to throw back. The only fish left were chub, herring and rainbow smelt, and no one was going to get rich off that.

As the *Retarius* cleared the Manitou shoals, Pete mumbled the first few lines of the sailor's prayer out of habit, then reached up to give three short tugs on the horn. A few minutes later he heard Andy do the same behind him on the *Murmillo*. There were quicker routes back to Cape Ernum, but this was the spot their youngest brother Charlie drowned when a summer gale appeared out of nowhere and swamped his leaky Mackinaw skiff. That was more than fifteen years ago, but for Pete and Andy the wound still felt fresh. Sometimes they talked about him like he was still around, a long-haired college kid always bugging them to take one of the big tugs out on his own. Charlie had just turned nineteen.

These channels had always been full of ghosts. In rough weather you could even hear the dead moan; some DNR study tracked the sound to water rushing in and out of the sandstone caves that pockmarked some of the islands, but generations of fishermen knew better. This stretch of Lake Superior between Duluth and Whitefish Bay was littered with three hundred years of wrecks; sailors didn't call it *The Graveyard* for nothing. Long before Gordon Lightfoot ever wrote that song, the Chippewa knew it as *Gitchi Gami*, the sea that never gives up its dead. Growing up here as a boy, Pete used to think that was all just silly poetry, but they never did find Charlie's body; the Manitou shoals were only a few hundred yards from the nearest landfall, a short swim, but all they ever found of Charlie was a single boot and the thick woolen heartwarmer his mother made him.

Pete watched the morning sun start to break over the treeline on Madeline, washing the top half of the wheelhouse in a warm orange glow. The sunlight felt good on his face, helping him to stay awake. The nights were starting to get colder; Pete had his old Navy peacoat buttoned all the way up and a thick wool hat pulled down to his eyes. He found himself daydreaming about June as the daylight painted silver streaks across the deep blue water of the bay. He wished she could be out here to see it. She always told him this was her favorite way to see the sunrise: from the water, on the way home.

He could still hear Jimmy and Johnny snoring down in the hold, a sound like sawing wood. No sense in spoiling their sleep; he'd call down a few minutes before they moored to wake them up and get the conveyor belt running to run the fish out. With their night, that shouldn't take long. With the price of diesel these days, Pete figured they'd hardly broke even; after firing up the smokehouse, dressing the fish and packing them in plastic, they'd really lose money.

Pete edged off the throttle as they passed the breakwater that separated Cape Ernum's pier and little marina from the bay. His stomach growled; he could do with some eggs, maybe a heap of whitefish livers on top. It had been a tradition since their father ran things to treat all the hands to a big breakfast after a night run. Pete smiled; with the way those two giants ate, he might as well take out a loan on the boats right now. He liked those boys. They had been telling stories all night about this guy everyone in town was talking about, Sam Davidson. Pete listened, wondering if he could help June.

There was a commotion on the pier. He saw a crowd of people on the dock. Maybe *mob* was a better word. There had to be two hundred of them, all milling about. He could hear a lot of shouting and arguing. A couple of them even were holding up signs, although he was still too far out to read them. What were so many people doing up so early? And what the hell were they doing on his pier?

Pete reached up and pulled the VHF receiver off its hook. "You seeing what I'm seeing?"

"Yah," Andy called back. "Maybe they think we snagged Free Willy or something." The line crackled for a few seconds before his younger brother came back on, laughing. "Barney and Phil over here wanna know if the Sons of Thunder finally got a fan base."

Pete searched around for his binoculars. "I don't think they're here for us."

"What do you want to do, big brother?"

Pete rubbed his chin. "Why don't you hang back a minute, let me go in and see what the hell's going on."

"Roger that. Hey, if it's some kind of crazy Greenpeace ambush, I'll come with the cavalry. Just like John Wayne," he said. "Only, at a top speed of nine knots."

Pete banged his fist into the bulkhead a few times. "You guys awake down there?" In a moment, he heard movement on the ladder behind him.

"Morning, skip," Johnny said, stretching his big arms and letting out a bear-like yawn. It only took him a second to see. "Hey, what the hell's going on over there?"

"Don't know," Pete said. "Rock concert, maybe." They were close enough now to see the crowd was in a semi-circle around a couple of men standing at the brink of the concrete pier.

"Hold on," Johnny said, rubbing the sleep out of his eyes. He was pointing at one of the two men backed up to the end of the dock. "That's *Sam*."

Now Jimmy was up the ladder too, making things tight in the little wheelhouse. "What's going on?"

"Sam could be in trouble," his brother said. "Come on." Both giants flew out the port hatch and slid down the ladder rail on their hands. Pete didn't know they could move that fast.

The boys helped Sam jump over the boat's gunwale and onto the deck.

"You're Pete Romack," Sam said, putting out his hand. "I hear you're a good man," he said.

Pete shook his hand. "That's what my wife says."

"Thanks for the rescue," Sam said. "It was getting a little tight down there."

"What do they all want?"

"Just like any crowd," Sam said. "Some come to listen, others come just to yell." He looked around the inside of the cramped wheelhouse. "Nice ship you've got here."

Pete smiled. "It's a *boat*," he said. "Fishing boat. Gill-net tug, to be exact."

"How's the fishing business these days?"

"Lousy," Pete said. "Well, looks like our pier is off limits, at least for a little while," he said. "Where would you like to go?"

Sam shrugged. "This is a fishing boat, right? So let's go fishing."

"Oh, no," Pete said. "We just got back from a night run. My guys are dead tired, and it'd take two hours to get back out there."

"How about right here, then?"

"Here?" Pete said. He started to laugh. "Mister, only thing you're going to hook here is a sunken log, maybe an old Chrysler." He pointed north past the tip of Hermit Island. "You got to head out to deep water to catch any fish."

"Humor me," Sam said.

Pete knew they had to be at least a quarter mile from shore to drop gill nets, and they were barely that. Reluctantly, Pete killed the engine and switched the knob on the VHF set to the topside speaker. "Boys, look alive out there. Get ready to drop 'em." He replaced the receiver and looked around for his brother's boat. With all the commotion, he'd forgotten Andy was still waiting out there. "You know, my brother's probably wondering what the hell is going on."

"I don't think so," Sam said, already pointing out one of the windows. Andy must have been watching; the *Murmillo* was only a few hundred yards off, and Phil and Barney were already at the winch motor, rolling off their blue nylon net into the water.

Pete heard the patient hum of the winch motor stop and he slumped back in his ripped chair. He should help the boys set the corks, but this close to the breakwater, he probably shouldn't leave the wheel. He motioned Sam to have a seat on the gear locker. "Take a load off, it'll be a while. We got coffee down below, it's not half bad."

But Sam kept standing. "Go ahead and pull your nets up," he said.

Pete glared at this stranger, waiting for a punchline to the joke. "Now I know you're crazy," Pete said, feeling his temper begin to slip away. Twenty minutes ago he was ready to go home and sleep until sundown. He took a deep breath, trying to choose the right words to explain how fishing out here works. After all, he didn't want to offend this man he'd only just met, this man who people swore could perform miracles. "Listen, this kind of fishing takes time. You got to play out your net, set your anchor lines, watch the spacing on your floats."

Sam stepped closer, his hand on Pete's shoulder. "Pull them up," he said. "Trust me."

Pete shook his head. This Sam guy was turning out to be some joker. "Mister, I'll humor you," he said, pushing off the chair and grabbing the VHF again. "Okay Johnny, bring 'em back up."

In a moment, he could hear the low chug of the motor again. But suddenly, Pete felt a rush of panic as the old steel hull began to creak. The whole boat had started to lean to one side. "Hang on, we've snagged onto something," Pete snarled; the last thing he needed from this little joyride were expensive repairs for a ripped net. "Probably that Chrysler I told you about." He shot out of the wheelhouse hatch and began to scale the starboard ladder. He froze midway down: it wasn't a car or a log at all. He could tell right away from the play on the net as it came up. The net was live. It *had* to be fish. In twenty years, he'd never seen anything like this. He felt something slap against the back of his head as he stood there in amazement; he realized some of the fish were jumping into the boat straight from the water.

There were dark clouds filling up the western sky; Pete shook off a sudden chill that had set into his shoulders. He wondered if it was just a knee-jerk reaction to the coming storm, a sailor's instinct, or if he was simply afraid of something else, and not ready to admit it. As the men on the deck worked the net, he studied the horizon some more; the weather was too far out on the water to be much of a problem for them, so close to shore. But Pete felt sorry for any small boats caught out there; this time of year, you never really knew what it'd become until it was right on top of you. Which was kind of how he was feeling right now. He didn't want to think too hard about this. He wanted to believe in a miracle right before his own eyes.

"Don't be afraid," Sam said.

"I was just worried about the storm," Pete lied, pointing out towards the deep water.

The winch motor struggled under the weight; the net was so heavy, it started to slip back off the roller. Pete lunged forward and reached over the side with both hands, trying to help pull it up. "Grab a gaff hook," he yelled. Johnny scrambled to find one of the long poles scattered on the deck. He sunk the end into the net, using his strength to keep the net from slipping back into the water. Sam was helping, too, grabbing the exposed net with both hands. Slowly, the net started to lift out of the water.

There was a storm brewing, all right. From Lucy's flying bridge, Tom watched the tall clouds drift in from the west, their dark bellies charred black like burnt marshmallows. The wind was picking up, and in the growing darkness the water had turned the color of old concrete. He was hoping it was just a passing squall left over from the summer, but he knew enough about the Graveyard to know you could never tell until it was on you: maybe you just got a couple hours of rain and a little tilt-a-whirl. Or maybe the waves got big enough to crack your hull in two like a sunflower seed and you found yourself on the bottom.

He felt a few cold drops of rain on his face. The old barometer Silas had glued to the bulkhead showed the pressure was dropping fast. He pulled out the marine two-way he'd hidden inside the lining of his jacket, checked the frequency and then turned up the squelch. "Lowey here. Put Judd on the radio."

"This is Judd. We're about three miles southwest of you."

"You see this weather coming in? Looks like it's going to get dicey out here."

"Guess this is what separates the men from the boys, Lowey. I thought you wanted to prove you could run with the big dogs? Do something more than catch speeders on the Rez?"

"I do," Tom said. "But you don't know the weather out here. This could get bad, real fast. I'm betting our mark has turned around already, headed back to Canada. In which case we're out here for nothing."

"You think it could get that bad, huh?"

"I don't know, Judd," he said. "But I'd rather not wait around to find out."

There was a long pause. "All right. Let's scrap it."

"Roger that."

He slid down the ladder, hoping his uncle had stowed some foul weather gear in one of the lockers down below. He hadn't seen Lazlo Hooker much since they shoved off that morning; the poor guy had been seasick pretty much since they cleared the dock. One thing was for sure: he wasn't much of a criminal. Tom took one last look around before locking the tiller and climbing down the ladder to the hold. He could hear Laz groan from one of the benches. There was the sour smell of vomit. Milk Dud was on the deck beside him, snoring softly.

Laz popped his head up. "Are we there yet?"

Tom rummaged around inside one of the stand-up lockers. "It might get pretty bad out here in the next hour or two." He could already feel the boat's hull lurch back and forth.

Laz tried to sit up, but only made it halfway before lying back down. "So what do we do when we get there?"

"What do you *think* we do?" Tom opened another gear box and pulled out a hand-held searchlight. "We use this to signal them." He clicked the light on and off, shining it right into Laz's face.

"Right," Laz said, shielding his eyes. "The *signal*. I like it. Very cloak and dagger."

Tom frowned. "Judd didn't say anything about you carrying a knife."

"No, it's an old expression from crime novels. Are you familiar with Mickey Spillane? Damon Runyon?"

Tom scratched under his ball cap. "I know *Matt* Damon."

Laz let out a whistle, looking around the deck like it was a jail cell. "We're going to have so much to talk about, aren't we? But money is money, and a job is a job."

"Listen, buddy—about that," Tom said, leaning on the edge of the table. "There's no easy way to tell you this, so I'm just going to tell you."

"Oh, let me guess," Laz half-laughed, half-moaned. The guy actually sounded amused, even though he was obviously in a lot of pain. "You're going to kill me. No, no, wait, even better, I've got it—you're a cop."

"Ding, ding," Tom said, nodding. "Bad River Tribal Police, at your service."

After a minute, Laz jerked upright, his eyes wide. "I was fucking *joking*," he said. "Are you serious? I can't go back to prison, you hear me? No way."

"Calm down. You're not going to prison, buddy. Listen to me: we've got bigger problems right now. As in *Act of God* type problems, you understand? We're both in trouble if this turns out to be a real blow. That's why we're turning around—make it back to land, or at least try to get out of the way of the storm. Here," he said, reaching into the locker and tossing one of the rubber rain jackets at Laz. "You'll need this."

"So wait, if you're some kind of cop, that means Judd—"

"Put the fucking jacket on," Tom said, already heading topside. "Then find the pants that go with it. I'm going to need you up there."

Laz picked up the jacket by the sleeve and looked it over before slipping it over his arm. "Cloak and dagger, after all. A real disaster flick."

Suddenly the world was an old black and white movie: even the water was coal now, churning out white froth. The waves would be up to the gunwales soon, and the rain was already as thick as television static. Tom knew the only thing to do was try to keep up speed and steer the boat straight into the waves; a big one hitting them broadside might turn them over, and then it was all over.

When he took the lock off the wheel, that's when he saw it: a wave—more like a wall of water—coming towards them from starboard. It was too late to turn into it. The old boat would probably break in half. He grabbed the life jacket he'd hung next to the wheel and slipped it over his shoulders, watching the wave roll closer. He thought about using the radio to call for help but there was no time. He pulled the cord on the EPIRB attached to the life vest out of instinct, and the white light from its beacon flashed into his eyes, blinding him.

He'd forgotten about Laz and Milk Dud down below. "*Get out of there,*" he yelled, banging his boot into the floor. "Get out—" But it was too late. The rogue wave must have been fifteen feet tall. The boat groaned like an old man and slowly turned over on its side. Tom was thrown from the deck and into the cold water. Everything rushed by him so fast. And for a moment, the world went black. He had no idea how long the sea had swallowed him, but when it spit him back to the surface, there was no sign of the Goosey Lucy, just the boiling grey water of Lake Superior all around him.

Pete had no idea how long he'd been sitting on the couch; he'd lost track of time, waiting for Sam to come out of the bedroom. When he looked down to check his watch he noticed someone had put a paper plate of the macaroni and cheese in his hands. He looked up and was surprised to see his house filled with people: some familiar, some strangers. He could see his brother Andy out on the porch, bent over the stacks of boxes, inspecting the island of misfit miracles.

"You should eat something," a voice said from the easy chair across the room. "Keep up your strength." Pete recognized Nick Demuz's face from the election posters. He was sitting with the talking octopus on his leg. "This is the weirdest thing I've ever seen in my life. Who the hell sent this?"

"You did," Pete said. "Your office did, anyway."

"Oh," Nick said, embarrassed. "Must have been Mildred, my secretary. Also, my wife."

Pete grunted; he didn't like the idea of people from town suddenly showing up in his house, especially politicians. "Just so you know, senator, I didn't vote for you." He found a clear spot on the coffee table in front of him to give the mac and cheese a final resting place. "I didn't vote for anybody. No offense."

Nick gave him an easy smile. "None taken. Sorry I've kind of invited myself in here. If it's any consolation, though, I'm not here for votes."

"Why *are* you here, then?"

"Same as you, I guess," Nick said. "I wanted to see a miracle happen, up close."

Out of the corner of his eye, Pete saw Sam coming into the room from the hallway. He looked tired, but he had a smile on his face. "She's going to be fine, Pete. You might want to give her something to eat."

Pete didn't say a word, he just rose like a mummy or maybe a zombie and started to run down the hall to the bedroom. He was scared to open the door, frightened that this was all just one more ruse, one more trick done with smoke and mirrors. He took a deep breath and pushed on the knob.

"*Close the fucking door,*" June screamed from inside. She was in front of the closet, putting on a shirt. Pete just stood there and stared at her naked body. When she realized it was him barging in on her, she smiled and dropped the shirt in her hands to the floor. She was beautiful. "Would you believe that nothing in this closet will fit me?"

He laughed, but he still felt like this was all some kind of dream. "How are you?"

She walked over and threw her arms around him. "So do you want the short version, or the long version?" She kissed him and leaned on his shoulder.

"The long," he said, kissing her again. "I want the long."

Lazlo Hooker could see a white light in the blackness, sparkling like a faraway star. He could feel himself drifting, no longer sinking but floating now, his arms out in an empty embrace, a ragged ghost haunting the void. His eyes felt heavy; after such an exhausting life, Lazlo Hooker finally felt ready for sleep. His skin started to warm as the light got closer. He had forgotten how good it felt to slowly drift into a deep sleep. He remembered curling up under the covers as a small boy and feeling so relaxed and satisfied, tugging the blanket over his chin. Sometimes his mother would read to him from the corner of his bed, the soothing rhythm of her voice helping him slip away into dreams. The light was closer now, looming like a harvest moon, bathing his body in its warm glow. He slowly reached into the darkness, stretching out both arms like a child yearning to be held one last time before sleep.

He could hear a voice calling to him in the darkness. *Listen to me*, the voice said. Now he could feel the tips of his fingers dip into the warm pool of light, then his wrists, then his mangled arms. *Listen to me*, the voice said again.

Lazlo shut his eyes, letting the sleep trickle into his head through his tired veins. He folded his arms into his chest and smiled. He opened his mouth in a last yawn, waiting for the voice to tell him more. He was ready to hear a good bedtime story.

The Parable of the Wise and Foolish Builders

Summer 2010

Red Otto is perched on his motorized scooter with your drawings in his lap, holding them up to the sunlight from different angles like he's trying to decipher hieroglyphics scrawled on ancient papyrus. The color in his craggy face is slowly draining back to normal; a minute ago it was boiling crimson from laughing so hard, the armrests on his bucket seat barely keeping the old man from spilling over onto the floor. You are standing in the lumberyard behind his hardware store, its wide aisles quiet as a tomb this early on a Tuesday, the morning sun already hot on your skin as it creeps over the mountain of fence posts stacked at the far edge of the yard. Red flips through the last few crumpled sheets, looking up at you with each flip while he shakes his bald head. "Okay, son, my guess is you want to build either a Roman catapult or a very, very, very large dishwasher. Am I close?"

"It's a stunt ramp," you say. "I'm jumping a dirt bike over the Little Missouri."

He bites his lip; he looks like he might slip back into convulsions at any moment. "Are you using a *magic* dirt bike? 'Cause that's the only way you'll make it over this contraption alive." He rubs his yellowed fingernail against the paper. "What the hell did you use to make these blueprints, son? Fingerpaints?"

"Um, well, that's actually magic marker there," you say, pointing at the first page. "And over there, I'm pretty sure that's crayon."

He holds it closer to his eyeglasses until they're almost touching. "Burnt sienna," he says like a man who knows his Crayolas. "You really went all out."

"I'm an idea man, Red." You always liked that phrase, *idea man*, but now that you've made it past forty and spent the last four months in rehab, you're pretty sure now that's always been just a nice way of saying *lazy*.

"Oh, an *idea* man." You hear him fight back a cough. "Well, then." He pulls out a handkerchief and spits into it. Then he turns the top piece of paper completely upside-down and gives it another look over the edge of his thick spectacles. He gives you a big nod, as if it all makes sense to him now. "Yep, I'd say these were definitely drawn up by an idea man."

You dig your hands deeper into your jean pockets. "So, Red—what do you think?"

"I think you suck at geometry, that's what I think." He rubs his chin. "But right off, I can tell you if you want to build a ramp this high, you're going to need more than just lumber and nails."

"Yeah? What else do I need?" You search for a pencil, eager for any advice.

"Start with an undertaker," he says, handing the papers back to you. "Then maybe look for a next of kin."

Your shoulders sink. "Thanks a lot." You stuff the paper into your shirt pocket.

"On the other hand, I guess there ain't no law against a grown man buying lumber," he says. "But this all seems like a pretty big job. You got your permits?" He looks up at you and sees the blank stare on your face. "You know, building permits? To build stuff? In the United States of America?"

"Oh, *those*," you say. "Sure did. First thing I did was go down to the—the permit place, you know, and get my hands on some building permits." You were never under the illusion that any of this would have to be *legal*.

Red spends about an hour taking you around the yard, showing you what cuts you'll need, what tools you'll need. Your lumber cart fills up pretty quick. He pulls your arm and makes you look him in the eye. "Okay, son, whatever you do, remember this one rule: *measure twice, cut once*."

You repeat it a couple times in your head. "Got it."

When you pay for the lumber and tools, Red follows you out to the parking lot, his scooter humming along. He sits there quietly and watches you load all the stuff into your pickup; it was years ago, but you can tell from the sharp gleam in his eye he hasn't forgotten the night when you broke into his shop and tried to get away with a cart full of power tools: sanders, drills, anything portable. The headline on the *Prairie Dog* that week said it all: *Drug Addict Raids Otto Hardware.*

You're surprised the old guy let you back in the store, much less help you.

You don't know quite how to tell him you're sorry; maybe you just don't have the guts. When you finish loading you stand there like a dummy and don't say anything. He's staring long and hard at you, like you owe him money. Which you do. "Okay, thanks for your help," you say finally, closing the gate on the pickup. "I'm going to go back to the river now, do a little building."

His eyes narrow. "Last time I saw you here, Lonnie, you were doing a little *stealing.*"

"I'm sorry about all that," you say, looking away. "I've kind of turned things around since then. I know you probably don't believe me. But it's true."

"Uh *huh*," he says, backing up to let a car get by. "So this is a comeback story."

He's still making fun of you, but at least he's not laughing out loud anymore.

When Annie Boone died, she left you a little money along with the house, an old Victorian set on a couple dozen lonely acres alongside the Little Missouri, outside of Nazareth. In her will she called the place Elephant Stomp

Farm, but you have no idea why. You know she got it from an old timer named Ole Simonson back in the 1980s when he kicked the bucket. You were only a kid back then so you barely remember him, but locals like Red Otto say he was the oldest man in the world. Snooping around the house, you believe it: you find a half a bottle of bootleg gin stuffed in the pantry, letters in a desk from a son writing from France in World War I, and a Sharps buffalo rifle from the 1800s hidden under the basement floor, a rusty cartridge still in it.

Annie died a dozen years ago but you only moved in here last month. *Moved in* might be the wrong phrase; after all, you don't have much to move, and you haven't really shifted anything from the way you found it, including the dust. There are two big bedrooms with post beds but you still sleep on the living room floor in your sleeping bag. Maybe you figure you don't deserve anything better.

You spent half Annie's money on rehab in Utah, which saved your life. They had you on Modafinil, which is the same drug they give narcoleptics. Detox from meth only takes a couple weeks, but they say withdrawal lasts the rest of your life. You still feel that old pull now and again, that sudden sting in your neck that wants to remind you that something's missing. When you left, they recommended you take on a long-term project to keep your focus, something physical, something gradual, something with a pay-off down the road that you can look forward to; some people take up painting, some people plant a garden in the backyard or hike part of the Appalachian trail. You knew your project right away; you are going to do what you always wanted to do, which is jump a dirt bike over the river. You came back to Nazareth on the bus and so far you've spent the other half of Annie's money on a second-hand Ford pickup, a few tools, and a whole shitload of lumber.

At some point, you're going to need to find a steady job; your math isn't very good, but you figure you've only got enough money to last the rest of the summer. Whether you've got the *guts* to last that long, well, it's going to take a lot more than math to figure that out.

There is a straightaway stretch of river along the property you figure is perfect for the jump. Red Otto threw in a tape measure for free with your first load of wood, so you know the river is seventy-six feet across at its widest, and probably anywhere from three to eight feet deep during the summer. Deep enough to drown, anyway. Across the river the far bank melts into the Badlands, the dusty mesas and arroyos stretching off into the horizon like an endless maze. You wade up to your knees in the cool water and look up, imagining yourself soaring high on your dirt bike—a new Kawi 450F you don't even have yet—and then landing on the high sloping sand on the other bank.

Maybe Red was right—it *will* take a magic dirt bike to pull this off.

When he threw in the tape measure, you thought he just felt sorry for you; now you realize he was hoping you'd give this up once you actually measured how far you'd have to jump.

You wake up on your first official day of building and the sky looks like rain, so you spend most of the morning sitting on Ole Simonson's porch, reading an old Time-Life book on laying concrete that you picked up at the Nazareth library. Every time you turn a page, you see another tool you don't have; even if you keep eating white bread and turkey Spam every day for the entire summer, you're still going to run dry of cash soon. You think about picking up some part-time work around here, but most folks in this town still remember the old Lonnie—the Lonnie from two years ago who stole power tools to support his habit and burned down his own trailer, and well—the interview wouldn't go so well. You don't blame them; you remember the old Lonnie, too. When you drive up to Watford City for meetings each week, you always stop at the Kum n' Go to fill up and play a couple scratchers, hoping for the best, but the most you've won so far is just another scratcher.

The rain clouds pass through by lunchtime, so now you are standing in the tall quackgrass on the riverbank, leaning on the tailgate of the battered old truck. You have your brand new tool belt strapped on, the one that smells like department store leather, its brand new tools shining in the sun as they dangle around your waist. The Time-Life book says the first thing to do is dig four post-holes for your main foundation, so you grab your brand new shovel out of the truck bed and look for a spot to start. On your first stab into the dirt, you hit a rock. After a few hours of hard work you are still on your first hole, but you do have a whole new collection of rocks, piled into a little stack. A thousand years from now, someone will study it as a product of a primitive culture.

As the sun starts to set over the Badlands, your back finally gives out. You're exhausted and when you look at the ground you realize you have nothing to show for it. Somehow, you still feel good. You notice two prairie wolves have come down to the riverbank to check on all the banging. When you look up, they scatter and disappear into the tall grass.

Red Otto is drinking hot tea from a ladybug mug and telling you this whole Daredevil Lonnie thing smells like a mid-life crisis. "I should know. I'm ninety-four years old," he says. "I've had three or four myself." He's taught you how to pick through a stack of two-by-fours to find the best pieces, so while he talks, you're looking at each board for any deep knots or splits and running your fingers along the grain to check for warping before loading the winners onto your lumber cart. You're getting pretty good at judging boards. If only people were so easy.

"Okay, Red," you say. "How do you know when it's a mid-life crisis?"

He sips his tea and thinks about it for a while. "When you find yourself doing something really stupid. Or saying something stupid. Or wearing stupid clothes. Or going out and buying something stupid."

"So, pretty much anything stupid."

"You got it." He sips his tea. "Like jumping over a river for no good reason."

"Hey, it's my dream, okay? I've wanted to do it ever since I was a kid."

"No offense, son," he says. "But a stupid idea that lasts for thirty years is still a stupid idea." He moves his scooter over to your cart and inspects the softwood boards you've chosen. "You're getting the hang of it, all right. Nice work, young man. You sure ran through your first batch of wood fast. Things are going well out there, huh?"

"I think so," you say. "It's looking more and more like a stunt ramp every day."

He sips his tea. "And you remembered the piece of advice I gave you?"

You nod. "Sure do. Cut it once, then measure it twice."

His puts down the teacup and sinks his head into both hands. "Please tell me you're not cutting the wood first, then measuring it."

"Oh," you say, laughing. "No wonder I used up all that wood so fast."

By August, you are the proud owner of four holes in the ground. You did have four posts up in the holes, but you mixed the concrete wrong and they started to sag every which way, like loose teeth. Then a twister tore through one evening and did you a big favor by ripping them out entirely, dropping them all over Galilee County. They found one in the community pool, another sticking straight up in the dirt parking lot in front of the Red Rooster like a hitching post for horses.

The next day you manage to set the concrete properly and level the posts, using the box beam level Red chipped in with your last batch of lumber. He says it's not as fancy as the laser levels he sells, but it gets the job done. "Lasers," he says, shaking his head. "What's next?"

You get a letter at the Simonson house from the county clerk. It's your first official piece of mail, but it reminds you about the property taxes you now owe. You're down to your last few hundred dollars.

You wish you had more to show for it.

R ed Otto is holding up a copy of the latest *Prairie Dog,* smacking the back of his hand against the headline. "Can't believe something like this could happen here, in this town," he says, shaking the paper in his gnarled hand. "Times change, I guess." You take the newspaper and scan the front page: seems the local hermit, Jan Olafson, hung himself in his cell down at the county jail a few days ago. You remember him; he used to work the meat counter at the SuperValu. He always appeared to be a bright and sunny guy, if a little odd.

"First I'm hearing about it," you say, handing the paper back. You only get into town about once a week, so pretty much any news of the world you get comes from Red. "They say if there were any witnesses?"

"Sheriff wasn't in at the time, but it says someone else was locked up in the other cell, some drifter. He must've seen the whole thing." Red seems shaken up about the suicide; as far as you know, he didn't know Jan Olafson that well, either. You think about telling him a little of your own story, the part where your addiction put you in a dark enough place to consider taking your own life, but you're not ready to talk about that yet. And you figure Red's probably not ready to hear it, either, so you find an empty cart and move it over to the stack of pine boards. Red trails behind you on his scooter; he's scratching at his smooth head and squinting behind his glasses now, like he's working on a crossword or a math problem he just can't crack alone. "Lonnie, tell me something," he says, licking his dry lips. "What makes a man want to take his own life?"

"I don't know," you say, inspecting a board. "Maybe he's in a lot of pain. Maybe he gets to a point where he feels like the world's better off without him."

"Maybe so," he says. "But I don't *understand* it. I mean, I never once felt like that."

You shrug your shoulders. "Not everyone makes it to ninety-four, Red." He seems a little more satisfied with that. You notice the store is pretty much empty again. "How's business going?"

He scratches the back of his neck. "You want the truth? Lousy. I'm too old to run this place anymore," he says. "Heck, I was too old ten years ago."

"Don't you have anyone to take over?"

"Got three sons," he says. "First one's retired in Arizona, second one runs a car dealership in Alabama. Third one came back from Vietnam back in '72," he says, taking a deep breath. "And jumped off a bridge a month later." He pauses to look up at the sky as if searching for something in the clouds. At least now you know why he's so distraught over the death of a stranger like Jan. "I got a few local kids working here part time, but they're not old enough to drink, much less run a hardware store. Place needs a working man, you know—someone with a little salt under their collar, if you know what I mean."

You nod, not sure what to say. "Well, I can't imagine Nazareth without this place." You go back to loading wood into your lumber cart. For the first time, you're worried you might not have enough money to cover it all. You reach for your wallet to make sure.

Red moves his scooter next to you. "Can I see your hands?" When you turn to face him, he sees the confused look on your face. "Your hands, hold them out. Come on, just humor an old man."

You put down the wallet and show him your hands. He leans closer, running his thumb over the new topography of coarse skin in your palm, the healed cuts and calluses you've earned over the last several weeks, making your skin rough.

He moves over your palm like he's about to tell you your future. After a minute, he sits back in his chair. "You're a working man, all right. You can always tell a working man from his hands." It's not until you are in the parking lot that you realize he was giving you a compliment. You just weren't ready for it.

You can hear the Harley coming from a mile away. You look up from the sheet of plywood you've got across a couple of sawhorses to see the glint of chrome from the highway. The August air is a shimmering curtain of heat, making you wonder if it's a mirage. You drop your tape measure and lift your T-shirt to wipe the sweat from your eyes. The bike slows down and turns onto the rutted trail you've pressed into the hard ground from running your truck back and forth between the main road and the river. There's only one motorcycle, but from all the sound it makes, you were guessing a whole gang was bearing down on you. The guy on the bike has long salt-and-pepper hair and a tangled beard. What some guys at meetings might describe as a *rough character*. You don't recognize him, but he rolls the old softail a few feet from the ramp, looking around the place like he's visiting an old friend. He sits there and looks over at you with a toothy grin. After revving the engine one last time, he kills the throttle and kicks out the stand. His face looks like it's been through a lifetime of direct sunlight and barroom brawls. A rough character, all right.

"Morning," you say, trying to figure out what the hell this guy wants. Your best guess is you still owe somebody money for drugs and they finally sent someone to track you down. "Can I help you?"

The stranger pulls off his dark sunglasses and bangs his boot on one of the beams you've set in the ground. "Let me guess, friend: you really, really love the Eiffel Tower."

"It's a stunt ramp," you say. Your hand is resting anxiously on the claw hammer in your tool belt.

"Oh," he says. "Then you're some kind of daredevil, am I right?"

"When it's done, we'll see. Some folks around here used to call me Daredevil Lonnie."

"Did they?" He seems amused. He spits into the ground. "Okay listen, Daredevil. I'm going house to house all along the Badlands here. You live around here long? You ever heard of a Sam Davidson?"

"Sure," you say. "Most folks around here know Sam."

"You seen him come by here lately?" He puts his shades back on and looks around. "I heard he might be heading out this way, taking a little stroll into the desert."

"Only soul I've seen out here in the last two months is you."

He nods, then drops to a knee to look at the ground. You can't tell for sure, but you think you hear him sniffing like a police dog. "Even so," he says. "I think he might be close." He gets back up and stares across the river, rubbing his beard. "I'll be back," he says as he starts to wade into the water. "Watch my ride. I shouldn't be long."

"Wait," you say, totally confused. "You're leaving your bike here?"

"There ain't no keys, but don't get any bright ideas," he says. "In other words, if you touch my ride, I'll kill you."

When he's halfway across, you gain a little guts. "Seems if you're leaving your bike on my property, mister, I should at least know your name." You realize this is the first time you've actually called this place *your property*, and you're pretty sure that's a good thing.

"You know what, go ahead and call me *Accuser*. Folks haven't called me that in a long time. I feel like going retro."

You've heard some aliases before, but that's a doozy, for sure. "Accuser? That sure is a weird name."

He yells back at you. "You're Daredevil Lonnie, and you're saying *my* name sounds weird? He gets up on the far bank and wipes some of the water from his chaps. He points a finger at the ramp, then cups his hands around his mouth to shout over. "Don't fart too loud on that thing, you might knock it over."

A few minutes later, he's disappeared over the first dune and into the desert. You expect him back soon, since he wasn't carrying anything with him, no food or water. But he doesn't reappear that day, or the next. Every morning, you walk from the house over to the river and pass the bike, which hasn't moved an inch. After a month goes by, you stop counting the days it's been sitting there, weeds tangled up through the wheels.

Red Otto doesn't operate on credit. You are sitting in his little office behind the cash registers, watching him drink his tea behind the cluttered desk. You need about ten more sheets of plywood for the ramp, a lot more double-sink screws, paint—and you haven't even gotten around to the road grater and roller you'll have to rent from him in order to work on the runway. "Way I figure it, there's only one solution to your problem," he says. You sag into the chair in front of his desk, expecting to hear another reason why you should drop this whole Daredevil Lonnie thing for good.

But instead, Red surprises you: he offers you a job.

"Could use an idea man around here, you know. Besides, you learned pretty much everything you'd need to know this summer," he says. "You know what you're doing. I taught you all the basics about wood, tools, and most important, common sense. That's more than I had when I took over for my old man here, about a million years ago. You can start tomorrow morning. Go ahead and take the supplies you need, and we'll find a way for you to pay me back a little on each paycheck. There's my pitch. So what do you say?"

You shake hands across the desk. "I won't let you down."

"I believe you," he says. "I know a good comeback story when I see one."

You get up to leave, but you stop in the doorway. "Hey, Red. You planned all this just like Miyagi in *Karate Kid*, didn't you?"

"Absolutely," he says, winking at you, "if I knew what the hell a Miyagi is."

Two figures crawl out of the Badlands. You are breaking for lunch—officially your last loaf of bread until you get your first paycheck from Red—and you're wondering if you're seeing another mirage, another trick of the late summer heat. You shield your eyes from the sun and move a few steps closer to the riverbank, but they're still over there, two shapes creeping on their hands and knees over the last crusted dune. They both slide on their bellies across the last few yards of packed mud before they hit the water. You're not used to seeing *one* person out here, let alone two. They make it to the bank at the same time, plunging their heads into the water. You recognize the weird biker guy from his clothes, even though they're ripped and torn now, covered in dirt and what might be blood—you can't be sure at this distance.

One thing's for certain: they both look like hell.

"*Hey*," you yell across the river, dropping your sandwich to cup your hands over your mouth. "Hey, you guys all right?" Accuser definitely isn't moving; his head has been dunked into the shallow water for a good minute now. You unbuckle your tool bet, kick off your boots and start to wade across the river. You see the other man start to rise, his shaggy brown hair caked with wet mud. When you get closer you realize it's Annie's grandson, Sam Davidson. He leans back on his haunches and coughs hard, wiping his dirty face with his forearm. "Help him," you call to Sam as you churn your legs faster; the biker guy's head is still in the water. You point. "He's going to drown."

Sam raises his head and pushes his hair out of his eyes. "You can't help him now."

You make it across the slow-moving river, swimming half the way. When you reach Accuser he's lifeless, and you push him over on his back. He's not a huge guy, but he sure weighs a ton. His eyes are open but stone cold. You feel for a pulse on his neck but there's nothing moving. You start beating on his chest, but still there's nothing. It takes you a while to accept the fact you're kneeling over a corpse.

You look over at Sam. "Did you kill him?"

"It's complicated," he says. "But I can tell you, it was either him or me."

You get up on your feet and face Sam. "Look, we need to call someone."

He seems so calm. "No need for that."

"What are you talking about? The guy behind me is *dead*."

"Wouldn't be too sure about that. Turn around, see for yourself."

You turn around and look back down at the man's body, but it's disappeared. Completely gone. There are no footprints leading here or away; even the imprint of his body in the mud is missing, like no one was ever there. "That's impossible."

Sam lets out a sigh. "Like I said, friend, it's complicated." Then he coughs up what might be blood or dirt—or a little of both. "You're Lonnie, right? Hey, you got any food over there?"

Your arms are folded. "Are you going to tell me what the hell is going on?"

"Later," he says, slowly getting up on his feet. "For now, help me across. I haven't eaten real food in forty days." He looks shaky, all right. You loop his arm over your shoulder and together you slowly wade across. You set him down in the shade behind the ramp and then find your cooler to make a couple of sandwiches. He wolfs them down like it's an eating contest. When he's done, he gets up by himself and dives head-first into the river, washing his face and hair. He comes back out a new man; he's got a smile on his face and almost no trace of being lost in the Badlands. Secretly you wish rehab could have been as easy as that, diving in a river and washing everything away. He comes back over to you and sits cross-legged in the sun.

"So, are you going to tell me what happened out there or what?"

He thinks for a while. "You ever have something you know you have to do, even though you don't really know why? Something you know your whole life you'll have to face?"

You put your hand on the ramp. "You're sitting next to it."

He stands up and kicks his wet shoe against one of the support beams, then tugs on a cross-bar with both hands. "This is solid work. You do all this yourself?"

"Yeah, but I had a lot of advice along the way. You know Red Otto?"

Sam nods. "He's a good man." He picks up your tool belt and tosses it to you. "Let me help you finish it up. Least

I can do. I know a few things about carpentry, from my stepdad." You've never had help before, but together, you work on the ramp the rest of the afternoon, shoring up the tower with extra support beams, then finally laying down the plywood track and nailgunning it into the tower. The hours go by quickly. While you work, you share all the memories you both have about Annie. Talking about things out loud feels good. As the sun dips behind the Badlands, you stand back and realize it's finally finished. You stand there a while in the orange dusk, running your hands over the beams, admiring the damn thing like it's one of the seven wonders of the world. "Getting dark," you say finally. "Guess we should pack it in for the day. Cold beers on me."

"Are you kidding? This is ready to go. I'm *pumped*. Let's do it now, what do you say?"

"Wish I could," you say, a little embarrassed. "But I don't have the bike yet."

He points to the softail half-covered by the grass. "What about that one right there?"

"No way. That's that guy's bike," you say. "Besides, it's totally the wrong kind of ride for this type of thing."

"Trust me, he's not going to be needing it anytime soon." He comes closer. "Listen, what have you got to lose? Cut the crap and just go for it. I say, move the truck, back that bike up all the way to the road, and let her rip."

"I don't know," you say, ambling over to the Harley and running your hand over the seat.

Sam is smiling. "Trust me, you're going to make it. I'm rooting for you. And that bike—well, I think you'll find it a lot faster than it looks."

You put your leg over and feel the tension on the clutch. You notice there are no gauges.

"What I'm telling you is, it's now or never." Sam comes over and puts his hand on your shoulder. "What the fuck, right?"

You kick-start the bike and it instantly roars to life. You roll it out of the weeds and let it rumble out to the main road. When you turn around, you stop and stare down the quarter-mile or so of dirt track between you and the river. It's flat and more or less straight, but it's no parking lot.

You realize this is crazy. "This is crazy," you yell to Sam, but the bike is too loud for him to hear, and he's too far anyway.

Sitting there, you realize it's *always* been crazy.

Sam is standing right at the base of the ramp, pumping his fist in the air and cheering. You feel different today. You don't feel the familiar sting of fear in your neck, a churning in your stomach. You sit there for a while, letting the motor chug. You are pretty sure that as long as you hit the ramp right, you probably won't die—the riverbed is soft mud and if you do make it over, the dunes on the other side are pillowed sand and scrub brush. At worse, you'll break multiple bones. Or maybe if you're lucky, break multiple bones, then drown. Or maybe. Or maybe.

Oh, what the fuck.

You open the throttle all the way and let go of the clutch, and the bike squeals on the pavement, leaving a black crescent moon on the highway. In a second you are already into third gear and halfway to the ramp, flying over the bumpy ground. You are officially Daredevil Lonnie and you've never gone this fast before in your life. You kick it into fourth, then top gear and lean forward until your mouth is kissing the handlebars. The bike hits the ramp and in another second you are airborne, weightless in crazy orbit as you feel the cool air rush past. The water shimmers below with the last rays of the evening sun. You can hear Sam behind you, whooping it up and clapping his hands as hard as he can. From this height, you feel like you can see the whole desert. From here, you are an explorer discovering a distant land for the very first time. Then the world suddenly starts to get closer again; you are falling so fast, but for the first time in his career, Daredevil Lonnie knows he can make it. You know you can handle whatever comes next.

Revelation

Winter 2013

I.

GOOD NEWS:
Everything you heard about heaven is true
When you die there is a white light that shepherds you away
There is a stairway made of swollen clouds
    and upbeat music that sounds a lot like early Elvis
        (that Gabriel blows a mean horn, man)
There is a big voice you swear is James Earl Jones
                narrating everything
But in paradise everyone speaks perfect French
even the angels
        At least they did when I was there
And would you believe everything comes in sevens: the
pearly gates, the streets of white glass
    the light fixtures

even this eight ball of sweet sweet meth
It speaks to me. It says: *Welcome home, Lazlo Hooker*
Welcome back to planet earth, home of hunger and noise
    known across the universe for its polyurethane and pas-
sive aggressive behavior
Welcome back you flaming HIV+ drug-addicted prodigal
son
Welcome home you sucker
      to your old stomping ground for letting people down

       I love you God
    but you make me want to shoot up
    Resurrection is your sickest joke.

II.

    Lord I have to tell you something
    you might have goofed
Tell the truth: did you even hear Amy Winehouse sing?
      Yes I've been black but when I come
back you'll

          know, know, know
Maybe you should have thought this one out a little more
Lord
    why choose me
    when you already own a perfectly good Rue McClana-
han

Maybe you should trade up
You know   someone with a little more *va va va voom*
How about bringing back a people person   like   Mister Rogers
How about Tony Curtis or Errol Flynn
          this job could use someone handy with a sword
And you obviously did not see Michael dance in *Thriller*
          or smell Julia Child's *lapin au vin*
     or hear Richard Pryor do the one about lighting himself
on fire
     or watch Gary Coleman in his 40s still doing his catch-
phrase at tractor pulls
Lord you might need to get a TV
What were you thinking when you took John Lennon for
good but
                         left me & Celine Dion & the guy from
Poison
Okay maybe I'm coming off a bit ungrateful Lord
After all you saved me from drowning
          but something about this whole thing makes me see
RED
I would like to say I'm sorry
                    but I won't
     besides
     I'm pretty sure Andy Warhol and Lucille Ball already
turned this job down
Maybe they figured out the big fat secret
     about Resurrection: when you come back from the

dead
    it's hard to find anyone down here who will listen
                  to you complain

III.

          But enough about me
    Let's talk about you, cruel world
I have BAD NEWS people
Because I see how it is all going to end:
               DRAGONS
No really
I see *fucking dragons* man
Okay   maybe that's the third hit off this eight ball talking but
    when you are born again
        your brain is made of comets
In my dreams I see dragons & winged lions & things you
don't ever see at the zoo
When I dream I see a leopard with feet like a bear and teeth
like a telemarketer
    (take *that* Charles Darwin)
When I dream I see a great white speckled bird with the
face of Johnny Cash
When I dream I see a big black horse
        charcoal eyes slowly smoldering like Michael Cor-
        leone looking at Moe Green in Godfather Two

Resurrection makes everything a sequel
I see the alternate ending, the director's final
cut
I see the Deus ex Machina
I see the killer hiding in the closet
I see all the Saturday matinee dreams of my youth
   but   framed in black
              like this hot acid afternoon

IV.

AND NOW
a brief history of the apocalypse:

You see   a long time ago there were special people
   like Nostradamus & Dick Clark & the Dixie Chicks
who got paid
        to dream out loud
They called it a Vision:
              step back while I demonstrate

I see the guy who shot Biggie
I see all the secret herbs & spices
I see the little jerk who stole your milk that day in the caf-
eteria

(Frankie Palladino)

I see how useless algebra really is
I see Helen of Troy was a solid eight & a half
      and did I mention the
                    DRAGONS

I see why Abraham Lincoln couldn't find his birth certifi-
cate
I see who really started the Spanish American War
I see what AC/DC really stands for
I can tell you the exact day when people stopped using
words like *trousers* and *swoon*
I see where they dumped the bones of Garcia Lorca
and why college kids don't like books
                          and how
                          they could defy gravity
                          if they just read Ginsberg out loud
I see Daylene finally making it to France
I see Daredevil Lonnie finally making it across the river in
one piece

                    I SEE SAM
He doesn't look too happy
      He kind of looks like Death
            a bizarro Sam: skin rough and pale like old concrete
            hoary grey breath bitter as wormwood
He's telling me to write all this stuff down
He says things like
                    I will kill them with death

(that's a direct translation from the French y'all)
He talks a whole lot about fear and burdens and chastity
and repentance and Satan and about

people he used to know in Philadelphia
I say   don't you have any good news
you know
something that will make folks feel better about the
End of the World
He thinks a moment and says
Tell them
I'm going to stand at the door and knock
If they hear My voice and open the door
I will come in
I try not to laugh
because even in Francais
that sounds an awful lot like an old Rolling
Stones song
But when I realize   He's way older than Mick Jagger
I feel pretty bad
besides   I'm pretty sure
it's only a metaphor

V.

I see Roxy too
And even though I am HIGH my heart sinks:
she is draped in dirty purple and scarlet, tired Queen of

slain martyrs
    the woozy Mother of the Dead
golden cup in her hand, limping around the walls of Zion
on a giant horny toad
       I try to chase her
But I only get close enough to see a word written on her
forehead:
               MYSTERY
I cry out: O Sam, O Prince of Peace
    I am afraid of what lies ahead for the rest of us, my old
friend
           if this is what happens to your own mother

VI.

Time's up
Tell them what they've won Lord
EARTHQUAKES
    (whoa)
        did you feel that one   cruel world
Get ready for tidal waves wrapped in lightning
           and hail the size of Mars
Global warming,   you're just an amateur:
    I see rabid tornadoes dancing on the bed
    I see volcanoes spitting out pancreatic cancer
    I see tsunamis turning hot deserts into heavy whipping
cream

I see puppies & kittens

    ignoring your beck and call

All the songs on the radio will be about suffering

All the channels will run disaster movie marathons

  think *Twister* meets *Armageddon* meets *Anaconda*

meets *Invasion of the Body Snatchers*

And I'm afraid

  there's nothing we can do:

It seems our beloved God of Yes

    has turned back into that ancient Lord of

No, No, No

The original God of salt and blood who told Abraham to slit

his own kid's throat

  and drowned 144,000 species in a heartbeat

    like brontosaurus and those cute little

horses

All Hail the return of the King of Bad Dreams, the grumpy

inventor of tough love

The God who used to go NUCLEAR on motherfuckers who

didn't listen

 You're lucky, cruel world

 You're too young to remember the God behind the seven

plagues of Egypt

  think *locusts* meets *boils* meets *darkness* meets *rivers

of blood*

 You don't remember the Creator who ground all those

cities into dust

    but trust me, I'm here to tell you

He's back

VII.

O what a great big tease you are Lord
              making everybody wait so long
              the only update they ever get is *soon, soon, soon*
Before I go
Here are some tips to prepare for Zion:
                        stock up on bread & milk
                        read more zombie books
                        Get yourself right with God

You better hide your old Metallica records and that DVD of
Ass Munchers 3
You better pack your own bowl
And for God's sake watch the language (for the record, *fuck*
and *shit* are not taking the Lord's
                        name in vain)
Take it from your old friend & Achilles' heel, Lazlo Hooker:
      if you see those shiny white gates of the Promised Land
          stay in line
          listen for the trumpets
          and watch your back;
You better hope your name is written in the right book
You better hope this story doesn't have
                  one of those surprise Endings

(you know   the kind where the hero = the killer)
You better hope you rolled a seven, brothers and sisters
    because if you crap out
        it's a long ride back
                down

The Last Supper

Autumn 2012

June lowered her head, watching her green Nikes churn back and forth over the frosted black asphalt as she started the long climb up the steep switch-backed hill to the Damascus bridge. It was a reflex from her high school cross country days: *lean forward from your hips, bring your arms in a little tighter, shorten your stride—and whatever you do, don't look up until you reach the top.* She felt the first rays of the morning sun warm the back of her neck; an old Pat Benatar rocker came on her iPod just in time for the climb, perfect for attacking steep hills. While she was laid up all those months, a bear in painful hibernation, her daughter Stacey had updated the thing with all kinds of new music—some kind of crinkled tinfoil confection called My Chemical Heroes? Gym Class Romance?—but to June, there was really no substitute for that hot pink bravado of 80s rock when you were a woman who needed to take a hill.

Halfway up the twisted hill, the chilled November air started to sear her tired lungs and she found herself shifting down to a choppy power walk. She was down to a crawl as she passed the old BRIDGE MAY BE ICY sign that had more bullet holes than paint. When she was a little girl, her dad would point to road signs like that as they drove past in his yellow Oldsmobile and he'd slow down and say something like, "See those bullet holes? The Dillinger gang came through here on the way to Manitowosh back in the thirties, on the lam from the feds." She believed him the first three or four times, but at some point she realized Dillinger must have sprayed machine gun fire at every sign in Jericho County. But it was the same pact they'd made with the tooth fairy and the Lake Superior monster: he'd pretend to tell the same worn-out stories for the very first time, and in return she'd nod attentively and listen, pretending to believe every word. She didn't mind the lie; she had always liked the fact her father took time to make up stories at all, even if they were warmed over leftovers.

About a hundred yards from the top, the cramps stabbed at both sides of her gut so bad she had to stop. She hadn't had breakfast yet; otherwise it'd be on display all over the blacktop.

When she thought about it, those tales were a lot like her dad: tough and dry around the edges from being left out too long, but warm enough to comfort. He'd been a fisherman all his life, just like Pete, just like her three brothers and pretty much any other able-bodied man born back then around Cape Ernum, a lost generation of boys taught to row a Mackinaw skiff before learning to walk. She wondered what giant whoppers the old man would be concocting now that Cape Ernum had actual federal agents running around, if he was still alive. He probably wouldn't have to try too hard to come up with a preposterous plot; after all, she could hardly believe the whole thing herself, and she was right in the middle of it.

She leaned on the railing for the last few yards, pulling herself along with her hands to make it to the foot of the bridge. She hated being this out of shape; a couple years ago she could fly up this hill and not break stride all the way to the top, glide over the overlook bridge and down the other side. On her best days she could keep going a few miles more, at least out to the parking lot at the Bad River Casino before finally turning around and heading home. Right now the stitch in her side felt like a meat cleaver twisting into her ribs; her knees had started to grind and groan like old floorboards put under too much weight. She closed her eyes, trying to sing along with the song lyrics—*midnight angel, won't you say you will*—but all she could manage was a sputtering wheeze. Considering she couldn't even get out of bed a few short months ago, just breathing in itself was more than a small victory.

It was hard to explain her emotions to anyone, even Pete; after all, how do you describe what it feels like to be living proof of a miracle? Ever since she got out of bed that morning like she'd simply awoken from a long sleep, everybody had been asking her, do you feel lucky? She never knew how to answer, but she did know *lucky* wasn't the right word. She felt humbled, she felt blessed. Most of all, she felt *loyal*. There wasn't any manual or guidebook, but she figured she'd been given this second life for a reason, and she didn't want to waste a minute of it worrying about the small stuff.

There were plenty of other things for her to worry about, anyway. Thanksgiving had been her idea, and at the time it sounded like a simple plan—get everyone together, make enough food to feed an army—but now with everything that was happening, it was looking more and more like a fiasco. Sam wouldn't hear of canceling it, though, even though he'd been close to being arrested. They were all being watched. The only place that felt safe these days was the old fishing camp on the outermost island, Oil Press, which you could only get to by a small boat, unless you were a black bear or an otter and could swim the icy channel. June wouldn't say this out loud, but in a way, it kind of felt good to be on the run. She liked that salty kick of adrenaline she got from being a part of something she believed in. She was looking forward to Thanksgiving, no matter where they had to have it. It was her favorite holiday, and she wanted to contribute in any way she could.

That, she definitely inherited from her mother—*when in doubt, cook something.*

She reached the top and immediately leaned against one of the bridge beams, trying to catch her breath. Usually when she made the bridge she celebrated by pumping her fists and dancing like Rocky Balboa, but not today; she stayed bent over, dry-heaving a couple times, both hands pushing in on her aching sides. If she didn't pass out, she'd limp another half-mile along the shore before turning around for home and a hot bath.

When she straightened up again she realized she wasn't alone: there was a white van parked across the double lane about a hundred feet down; there were two men in long coats standing and looking out at the morning mist that shrouded the islands. June rolled her eyes; she didn't have to see the government license plate to know they were watching her again. These guys usually came in pairs: same bad haircuts, same steel-toe shoes, same smiles right out of the high school yearbook. She wondered where all the female agents worked; it sure wasn't Wisconsin. If she ever got followed by two women in dark coats and a van, she'd probably faint from surprise. As she walked past the van, she didn't recognize these two—but they all seemed interchangeable anyway, manufactured at the same douchebag factory.

"How's the cancer doing, June?" the short one said, in a peppy tone that suggested they might be old friends. "Still in remission?"

She had grown used to dealing with these guys. "Totally gone. Thanks for asking," she said with an automatic smile. It was hard to remember this was her own tax dollars at work, these men spying on her morning run. "Totally healthy, thanks to Sam. Why don't you two clowns write that down somewhere? *Subject June Romack stated she was cured of pancreatic cancer by Sam Davidson.*" She spit on the pavement between them. "I'm assuming that's why you're up so early, following me."

"Following you?" The other one slapped his gaunt face in mock surprise. "We're just a couple of local guys, out here enjoying the view."

She looked at the unmarked van. "Yeah, if you're local, I'm a unicorn."

"Oh, we're from around here, you bet," the short one said. "We're from right here in—hey, Sully, what's the name of this podunk town again? Cape Something?"

The taller one sipped his coffee. "Cape Bullshit, if you ask me."

"That's it, Cape Bullshit. Right in the heart of Jerk-Off County." He turned towards the open water, taking in a long breath like a tourist. "Home of that miracle fish smell."

"You guys need to get out more," she said, backing away. "Happy Thanksgiving."

The one the fat guy called Sully saw she was about to leave and put down his travel mug on the metal railing. "We're interested in talking to you sometime," he said in a voice that surprised her, probably because he sounded almost like a human being. "We'd like to talk with Pete, too."

"Yeah," the fat one laughed. "We'd like to talk to Pete and Andy and Judd and all the rest of the Little Rascals, too. They can put together a talent show to save the clubhouse— or to stay out of jail."

"That's enough," Sully said, turning to scowl at him. His voice grew a little softer. "Seriously June, I know you think we're the bad guys, but we're here to help. We want to help you and Pete, before anything goes too far and someone gets hurt. Or worse," he said, taking another step closer to her until he stood right on the yellow line. "Let me ask you a question. How much do you love your husband?"

She jumped back like she'd been bitten by a snake. "Excuse me?"

"Because I have to tell you, Pete has fallen in with some pretty bad dudes. Do you realize how much danger he's getting into, following this Sam Davidson around? Listen, why not just take my card," he said, reaching into his coat and pulling out a wallet. "Everyone needs someone to talk to once in a while."

Out of instinct, she took the card from his hand before backing away. It was the same unexplainable instinct whenever she accepted flyers in front of the Walmart from strangers even though she'd never want anything they were hawking. She looked down at the business card in her hand; it had a tiny eagle seal and his name, Patrick Sullivan, over the title *Special Agent*. "Wait," she said, cupping it in her hand. "What kind of danger are you talking about?"

He rubbed his forehead. "I'm surprised. I thought you knew," he said. If this guy was acting, he was putting on a command performance. "Things are pretty bad. Sam's leading Pete into some real trouble. Ask your husband, he'll tell you all about it."

"You're lying."

"Am I?" He backed off a step, digging his hands into his pockets. "Enjoy the rest of your morning run. And congratulations on beating the cancer, June, really. Truly is a miracle. Your doctor told me he'd never seen anything like it in thirty years of medicine. You know, only a handful of other people like you beat that one. I know, I checked the statistics. Of course," he said, tilting his head, "somehow those people got better without their own personal healer."

"I'm not the only one he's healed," she blurted out. "Ask anyone around here."

"That's what we hear," he said. "We're going to look into those stories next. One thing we're finding out for sure is that faith is one hell of a powerful thing." He sipped his coffee again. "Can be a dangerous thing, too."

She'd heard enough. She turned and started to run the rest of the way across the bridge, stealing a look behind her a couple times. She backpedaled and watched them climb back in the van and head off in the opposite direction, back towards town.

"You have a Happy Thanksgiving, too," the shorter one yelled as they drove off.

She realized she still had the card in her hand; her fists had been balled up for a while now, and it had gotten trapped between her fingers. The sweat on her skin had cooled, making her shiver. Her legs ached with the first few steps back on the road. She tried to find a rhythm again, but her head suddenly felt like it was full of sludge, making it hard to concentrate on anything, much less her breathing.

They had been hovering outside the window all night, a coven of drunken witches taking turns pressing their fat, crooked faces against the cold glass, shooting nasty glares at her through the clouded porthole of the Captain Flint. *All they need is a boiling cauldron to stand around while they cackle,* Veronica thought; now she could hear them chanting her name, almost like they were casting a spell—*Ron-nie, Ron-nie, come on out Ron-nie*—waiting for her to come out from the bar and face them in the empty darkness of the street. It was past closing time on a Tuesday and the Flint's last customers left an hour ago, but Veronica kept wiping down the taps with a bar towel and checking the caps on the well bottles for the hundredth time, hoping the three tanked-up sirens outside would lose interest and just go home. She thought about calling a friend to come get her—or at least walk her the fifty yards to her car—but she realized she didn't have anyone to call, not in Cape Ernum at two in the morning, anyway. She could wake up the sheriff, or even the judge, but the fish-witches outside would probably just disappear and show up to surround her house later anyway, tossing their half-empty tallboys against her door. This was a small town, too small to avoid people forever, especially Delmina Gorman and her fishwife cronies, Jackie and Gerd.

Toil and trouble, Veronica grumbled under her breath.

Two weeks ago, she had made the mistake of sleeping with one of her regulars, Ben Gorman. It was a mistake for at least three reasons: first, she knew Ben was married; second, she knew he would never keep his mouth shut; and third and most important, she already knew just how lousy he was in bed.

Why was it that no matter how old she got, parts of her life were always going to feel like high school? Back then, she never got scared of the packs of girls out for revenge, and she wasn't really scared now, either; she was just tired of having to walk around this town with a scarlet A etched on her forehead, because she happened to be a woman who got lonely once in a while.

Sleeping with Ben was no crime of passion, it was more an act of middle-aged desperation, a cave-in of sadness. Every single part of this man smelled like fish—his wispy hair, his sunken chest, his dried fingernails—and when he was on top of her and close to coming, he kind of flopped around, too, his arms and legs quivering like a big fat walleye in its death throes as it slaps around on the deck. Veronica suddenly laughed out loud when the image came to mind, but right now she felt too sorry for Delmina, who somehow had been married to the man for twenty years without going insane.

"Ron-nie, Ron-nie," the fish-witches kept chanting outside.

Double toil and trouble, Veronica mumbled. Maybe she shouldn't feel too sorry for them; after all, she was the one who was going to be alone on Thanksgiving again, eating a Lean Cuisine in front of the TV. She just wanted to go home, fucking fish-bitches be damned. Finally she grabbed her coat off the rack, slapped at the row of light switches at the end of the bar and headed for the front door. She stepped outside and started immediately for the marina parking lot, not even bothering to waste time locking the door behind her. She was hoping she could make it to her car before the three fish-witches built up enough steam to do something stupid. Veronica kept a little league bat in the car, which had always been perfect for warding off drunken men, and more importantly, their drunken wives.

"There's the Jezebel," Jackie yelled out. "There's the bitch who fucked your man."

Veronica hurried past the three of them, fumbling around in her bag for her car keys. "You're all drunk," she called behind her. "Just go home already."

"Hey, Delmina's gottarightobe drunk," Gerd said, her words all glued together as they came out of her mouth after a whole day of beer and shots. She was holding out her arms for balance like a trapeze artist, listing to one side like she'd fall off the rope any second. "And she *can't* go home, thankstoyou, Ronnie. Youfucking. Home. Wrecker."

Jackie and Gerd then turned to Delmina, waiting for her to add something. After a long pause, the short, stout woman finally belched and said, "She's a slut."

"Yeah, that's it, you're a *slut*," Jackie said, jabbing her finger in the air. The three of them started to catch up behind

Veronica, spaced out in some kind of weird wedding train. "And you know what we do with sluts around here?"

"Yeah, you know how we treat sluts around here, right?" Gerd said.

Veronica cursed as she dropped her keys on the pavement. She dipped down quickly to pick them up again, not breaking stride, her feet moving even faster now. "I don't know, buy them a trip to Cabo?"

Jackie howled. "Oh, we got ourselves a fucking comedian."

"Yeah, a fucking *comedian*," Gerd said. "Right, Delmina? She's a comedian, right?"

Delmina let out another belch. "Slut."

Veronica made it to her battered Hyundai and slid around to the driver's side, trying to find the right key in the dim light of the sodium lamps that were spaced out along the silent docks. Out of the corner of her eye, she noticed there were three or four figures slowly ambling up the dock, almost as if they were ghosts or sleepwalking, hauling mounds of gear on their shoulders. They were probably coming off a night run. Veronica cursed under her breath; that's all she needed, a few grumpy fishermen to come along and make this movie even worse. *The Revenge of the Fish-Witches* was quickly turning from a guilty-pleasure comedy to a cheap horror flick and for the first time tonight, she was getting a little scared. She wanted to be home already. Finally, she felt the right key in her fingers and stabbed it into the lock. Veronica turned her head as she pulled on the door handle, watching the three women get closer to the back of her car.

Just as she unlocked the door, suddenly there was an ear-piercing crash that made her duck down out of instinct. She got up again and saw the rear window of her car was completely shattered.

"That was a *rock*," Jackie said, slapping hands with Gerd. "You hear that, bitch? I just threw a fucking rock at you."

Veronica still felt a high-pitched whining in her ears from the impact. She leaned over and waved her hand around in the chilled air where the glass used to be, as if it was a simple magic trick to make her windshield disappear. But when she peered down into the car she could see shards covering the backseat, a rumpled blanket of raw diamonds. She just stood there frozen, still in shock. "You broke my window."

"Yeah, but she was aiming for *you*," Gerd said, still holding her hand up in vain for Delmina to give it a high-five. "Bitch who fucks your man gets a big rock thrown at her, right?"

Delmina chugged the rest of her beer. "Slut."

Jackie and Gerd were both going back over to the little park on the edge of the marina to find more stones.

Veronica still hadn't moved when the men from the docks came up behind her. "What the hell is going on here?" she heard one of them say. It was an unfamiliar voice, but at least it sounded like it might be on her side. Two of the men came closer, and she knew it was the giant Thunder twins before she even saw them up close; they were so big they blocked out the lamp light coming from behind. They dropped the fishing gear they had slung over their shoulders and stood there looking around, trying to get a read on the situation. Veronica recognized the other one as he stepped closer to inspect the damage to the rear window.

It was that preacher guy, Sam Davidson.

"Hey, we know you," Jackie yelled. "You're that holy man everyone's talking about."

"Oh, we got one for you tonight, mister holy man," Gerd said, pointing at Veronica. "We got a real live adulteress, in the flesh. Go on, smack her forehead and give her some of that holy spirit like they do on the TV."

"Yeah, on TV," Jackie added. "That's what they do to bitches who sleep with your man."

"You don't say," Sam said, scratching at his scraggly beard. "And who is she supposed to have slept with?"

Jackie waved the rock in Delmina's direction. "Her man. Ben Gorman."

He turned to Veronica with a smile. "This true?" She shrugged her shoulders, looking away into the night. She didn't need a lecture from some preacher; she might choose the rocks over someone telling her once again everything wrong with her life. For some reason Veronica couldn't comprehend, Sam pulled a piece of colored chalk out of his vest pocket and crouched down to start scribbling something on the pavement. Standing behind their leader, Jimmy and Johnny both folded their arms and smiled a little to each other, as if they were settling in to enjoy a show they'd seen before. She couldn't see what he was drawing—maybe a chalk outline for a dead body or something like in those crime thriller movies—but whatever he was doing, it made the fish-witches curious enough to stand still for a moment.

"Ben Gorman," Sam said in a loud voice, not looking up as he wrote. "And I take it you ladies have already thrown rocks at *him*?"

Jackie stopped tossing the stone up and down in her hand. "Well, no."

Sam nodded, still drawing. "And he's done this before?"

"Well, yeah," Gerd said, turning the toe of her boot in the ground. "Plenty."

"Well," Sam said. "I'm not a relationship expert or anything, but it seems to me you might be blaming the wrong person here."

"But she's a *slut*," Jackie said. "She's the one who lured him into sin. Right, Del?"

Delmina drained the last drops of her tallboy onto the pavement and tossed the can away. "Ben's a slut." When she said that, the last gusts of the wind seemed to leak from the sails of the other two. Delmina spat on the ground. "Come on, girls, let's go home." One by one, they turned and walked slowly back up the street, disappearing into the alley behind the Captain Flint. A few moments later, an old Trans Am rattled out onto the street and up the steep hill, a lone red tail light disappearing over the rise.

Sam got up, wiping his hands on his coveralls. "Are you all right?" he said to her with a soft air of genuine concern.

She looked down at her own arms, as if she half-expected to see stab wounds or evidence of grazed gunshots.

He looked down the street. "I guess your firing squad up and left."

She folded her arms across her chest. "This is the part where you tell me I should get right with God or something," she said, letting out a nervous laugh. "You're going to start the lecture by saying something like, *Ronnie, I'm really worried about your soul.* That's what you're about to say, am I right?"

"I wasn't worried about your soul," Sam said. "You seem like you have a good one."

"Yeah," Jimmy said sleepily. "We were just worried about you getting beaned with a rock. Although I see a Louisville Slugger in there with a few dents in it, so I guess it'd be even money."

"Their aim kinda sucked," Johnny said, looking at the car.

She felt herself softening a bit. "I guess I owe you one," she said to Sam. "I hope you don't think bad of me—about the whole Ben Gorman thing, I mean." She had heard all the stories about what this guy could do, but it was different standing next to him. "I know you're the local holy man and all."

Sam shrugged his shoulders. "I'm not condemning you for anything. I just think you can do a lot better than Ben Gorman." He smiled, then squeezed her shoulder a little. His touch made her feel warm, a low voltage electricity slipping over her skin. And with that, the three men drifted off into the darkness towards a pickup truck parked down the street. They dumped their gear in the bed and rumbled up the hill, the diesel echoing.

Standing there, alone again, Veronica wondered what had just happened. Maybe it was the fresh kick of adrenaline finally wearing off, but this whole episode all felt like a rushed dream—that is, until she looked at her busted window again. But she couldn't help but think the movie had changed one more time, maybe to something more uplifting this time, something with a story a little more worthwhile. She couldn't put her finger on why, but she felt *good*, good enough to forget about the damage to her car. She wasn't ready to admit a simple touch from a stranger would do that. She knew all about him, but she was nowhere near prepared to use all those hokey words like *salvation* and *redemption* and oh Lord, *being saved*. But it'd been a long time since she'd been part of a story where things had a good chance to turn out all right.

He was being followed this time, he was sure of it. Judd kept his eye on the rearview as he dipped his softail into a supermarket parking lot, pretending to look around for an empty space. A few seconds later, he saw the green Prius dart past behind him in the mirror. He waited a few seconds before slowly turning his head and picking it up again in the slow stream of cars, but the car just disappeared down the street with the rest, not turning or slowing down.

Judd leaned back in the saddle for a moment, looking up at the clear sky through his mirrored shades and shaking his head. Everything was closing in on him, even the mid-day traffic on a Tuesday. *Maybe I'm just slipping,* he thought to himself.

After all, would anyone really be tailing him in a Prius?

He kicked into gear, rolling the throttle a couple times before letting out the clutch. He pointed the bike towards the back of the massive concrete lot, searching for a rear entrance. He was going to be late again, but one thing he'd learned about undercover work was that keeping a schedule was a sure way of getting caught: cops are on time, felons are not. Watching your back was a full-time job. This was just his usual sit-down with Matthias anyway, and his old friend Matty Ice would probably understand.

He cruised through some back alleys until he found the right street, then circled a couple times just to make sure he'd be coming alone. This was a new drop spot, all the way down in Ashland; usually he met Matty Ice at some roadside joint, laundromat or abandoned barn a lot closer to Cape Ernum. This was a bar without a name in Ashland's old warehouse district. Judd backed up the bike until it nudged the curb and then he killed the engine. He took one last look around the deserted street before standing up and shaking off the cold. Judd headed inside the bar, re-turning the bartender's nod and headed for the door in the back with a piece of notebook paper taped to it that read *OFFICE*.

Judd opened the door expecting to see Matty like always but when he slipped inside the dim room, a strange voice greeted him. "Nice of you to join us." Judd froze as he looked around the room: there were a half-dozen men sitting around the table, all looking up at him. Matty was there all right, staring down at the table as he pushed a Styrofoam cup of coffee back and forth in front of him. Matty Ice didn't look too happy, but then again he didn't get his nickname back at Quantico for wearing his heart on his sleeve.

Judd closed the door behind him and moved towards the empty chair next to Matthias. "So is it my birthday or something?" he said as he sat down next to the only familiar face in the room. No one said anything right away. "Okay then, let me guess: it's Take-An-Asshole-To-Work day."

"Easy," Matthias said, clearing his throat. "Task Force wants to get the latest on all the fun you're having up there in the islands, all by your lonesome. I would've warned you, but you don't like to use the phone, remember?"

"Some Task Force," Judd said as he slowly shook his head, as if he'd never heard the words together before in his life. "More like a sad joke. There's one guy working his ass off to take down the bad guys, and then a whole bunch of dumb asses who sit around a table." He reached into his vest for a crumpled pack of cigarettes. "Listen, *Task Force*, I don't have time for this crap. Sackett out."

There was this white-haired old goat across the table from him, drumming his gnarled fingers on the table impatiently. "So this is your man inside we've heard so much about: Special Agent Fourchette," he rang out, much too loudly. "Oh boy, I feel better already."

Judd closed his eyes. "Don't use my real name, asshole. You call me Judd." He turned to Matty. "What is this, amateur hour?"

"A man drowned because of you," Conway sneered. "I'd call that amateur."

Matthias put out his hand to restrain Judd while he drew a deep breath. "This is Mr. Conway, he's the district judge up in Jericho County." Something was off in his voice, like he was reading off cue cards. "As you know, the Task Force is a joint cooperation between state, local and federal law enforcement agen—"

"Spare me the brochure," Judd interrupted, checking his pockets for his lucky lighter. "It's nice to have so many folks interested in our little operation all of a sudden." He looked at the faces around the table one more time. "We got some backwater judge sitting in, even. Tell me, we got the Boy Scouts represented here? How about the Wisconsin chapter of AARP?"

There was some balding geek at the end of the table in a shirt and striped tie who must've been in charge of this little cabal. "Pat Sullivan here, Judd. Good to finally meet you. We read all your sitreps—we just want to talk to you face to face, get some fresh intel."

"Oh, that's bullshit. I know why you're all here," he said, lighting up a smoke. "You want to move on Sam Davidson."

"Please don't smoke in here," Sullivan said. "And forgive us for finding the apparent leader of a criminal organization interesting."

Judd sprang up. "You've got it all wrong. Sam Davidson has nothing to do with the Sicarii. It's all in my reports," he said, pausing. "Sam isn't involved in any of it."

Conway sniffed. "Sounds to me like you fell in love with the guy or something."

"Fuck off," Judd said, almost ready to reach across the table. "Sam's the real deal."

"So you've seen him do miracles," Conway said. "You've seen it with your own two eyes?"

"I was there when he made that teenage kid walk, damn right."

Conway let out a long whistle. "Sounds to me like you've got an agent going off the reservation, Mr. Sullivan," the old man said. "Next thing you know he'll be running around in the woods singing Kumbaya with the rest of these hippie nuts."

Judd had had enough of talking to the peanut gallery. He knocked the chair over as he lurched for the door, taking a huge fuck-you puff off his cigarette and blowing the smoke into the air. He'd done his job, and he'd done it well: he helped take down the Sicarii. Now these assholes wanted to take down Sam too, pin all this on him just to get rid of him. Judd wasn't going to follow along with that. He didn't have many real friends in this world, and Sam was definitely one of them.

Matty came out a few minutes later, running a hand through his short hair. "You really screwed the pooch in there, you know that."

Judd shrugged his shoulders and took another long drag.

"I need to ask you a question," Matty said hesitantly. "And I need a straight answer. Okay?"

"Anything for God and country," Judd said, smiling. "You know that."

"They're planning a raid for Thanksgiving, taking everyone in at once—the Sicarii, Davidson and his followers, the whole magilla."

Judd tried to cover his surprise by looking away. "Didn't Waco teach them anything? Ruby Ridge? It'll just be another disaster, more people getting killed."

"They're not changing their minds on this one. Everyone's on board, except you. They need to know a time when everyone's going to be in the same place." He swallowed hard. "Do you know their plans for Thanksgiving?"

Judd bit his lip. "I don't know yet," he said, automatically feeling bad for lying to his friend. He knew they were going to all have Thanksgiving together out on Olive Press Island, away from all the crowds now thronging Cape Ernum to see Sam, but he wasn't ready to tell these guys yet.

"Listen, they've got another source supplying information on the location," Matty whispered. "They thought you would corroborate it. There's an old abandoned fish camp on Oil Press Island that the Sicarii use from time to time for meetings and shindigs, right? You know it?"

"Wait, another source?" Judd raised his eyebrow. "Who?"

"Sullivan won't say, but it sounds legit. Definitely someone else on the inside." "Listen, you've done a lot of good work here," he whispered, leaning against the brick wall. "They're going to take it the rest of the way whether you like it or not. It's not up to us anymore, understand? They're going to rush that island, with or without you."

"Then if it's all the same to you, I'd like to see this through," Judd said. "Besides, I know that island better than anyone you've got."

Matty rubbed his chin, then slowly nodded. "I was hoping you'd say that. Okay, I'll talk to Sullivan. Just remember which side you're on."

"What the hell is that supposed to mean?"

"Ever since this Davidson guy came along, you've changed. I see it in your face every time you turn up. Your job is to take down the bad guys, that's it. Those assholes in there? They're a little worried you might've gotten too close on this one. They don't want you warning anyone about this raid." He put his hand on Judd's shoulder. "All I'm saying is, don't forget who you work for, all right?"

"God and country," Judd said, tossing the last of his cigarette into the gutter.

"That's the spirit," Matty said, slapping Judd's arm. "God and country."

"What are you going to do when this is all over? You've got some time coming to you, probably a promotion too if I have any say in it."

Apostle Islands

"Honestly? Got my eye on a little piece of land," he said. It was another one of his secrets that had been locked away for so long: there was a little farm near where he'd grown up, a place called Hinnom Valley. He'd always had these wild dreams of being a farmer, and now he was yearning for the idea of solitude and peace more than anything. "You know, going to grow some vegetables, maybe raise a few chickens and milk goats."

"Wow." Matthias perked up. It was the first he'd ever heard of the plan, but he was happy for him. "Brussels sprouts? I love me some brussels sprouts."

"You got it," Judd said, smiling as his friend shook his hand one last time before heading back inside. Judd stood there awhile on the empty street. Matty was right about one thing: he *had* changed. He'd gone into this thing about as gung-ho as a man could get, but now he was coming out the other side with plenty of surprise baggage: a conscience, for one. This job used to be so simple: good and bad, right and wrong. Deep inside, he had nothing but contempt for all the bikers and militia members he'd pretended to befriend. But Sam was different. He'd tried hard to find the cracks in Sam and expose him as just another fraud. But he hadn't found any, and it scared him more than anything.

He slid back onto his chopper and steeled himself for the cold ride up Route 13, back to Cape Ernum. The sun was high but there had been a sharp wind coming off the water all morning. Pretty soon it'd be too cold to ride, even for him. Out of the corner of his eye he saw the green Prius hiding behind a delivery truck on the next block.

So he *wasn't* slipping after all—at least not when it came to being followed.

When it came to following others—well, everything was starting to slip.

Veronica was using the slow night at the Flint to put up the last of the Thanksgiving decorations: cardboard turkeys with blunderbusses and buckled hats, strings of plastic pumpkin lights, orange and yellow frills taped along the bar. There was only one customer in there, old Carl Feeney, and as long as you changed out his beer for a fresh one now and then, he didn't need any attention at all. Veronica was by the front window, balancing on a stool, trying to hang mini-cornucopias from the rafters when the last person in the world she ever expected to walk inside this place came right in the front door.

"Hey, Ronnie," Sam said casually. "Have time to make me a quick drink before I go?"

She climbed down, glancing nervously at Carl. "What can I get you?"

"Something from the well," he said, leaning on the bar. "Doesn't have to be fancy."

George drank the last of his Huber in one gulp and dropped a couple bills on his corner table, then hurried out the alley door, keeping his eye on Sam the whole time. Veronica knew he was headed straight for the judge's house, midnight or not.

"Listen to me, I've been all over town looking for you," she whispered, even though with George gone the rest of the bar was empty. "You're in a lot of trouble."

"Story of my life," he said, taking a long sip of his drink. "Hey, this is good."

"Seriously," she said, drawing closer. "Key Conway, the judge? He uses this place as his personal office. He says some things," she said, pretending to wipe down the bar as a couple walked past the windows. "And I hear some things. I couldn't make out everything, but they're planning on arresting you on Thanksgiving. Someone told them where you all are going to be—one of the islands, right? They want to get you all in the same place, away from people. So they're going to raid the island and arrest everybody."

"Wow, sounds like a real plot," he said. "Sounds like a Keanu Reeves movie."

She slapped the bar. "It's all true, I swear. I'm not making it up. I owe you for that night, you know—for saving my ass."

Just then, Jimmy Thunder poked his head in the door, his brother right behind him. They both had hard faces. "Hey Sam, what are you doing in here?" Jimmy looked around the place. "Could be dangerous."

"Belly of the beast," Sam said. "Pete and Andy ready to put out for Oil Press?"

Jimmy nodded. "Picked up the turkeys at the IGA just now. June said she wants to make a roast to go with the turkey, so we got that, too."

"And lots of mashed potatoes," Johnny said from outside.

Sam laughed. "You guys are making me hungry already. Meet you on the dock."

Jimmy still hovered at the door. "It's not safe to stick around here."

"I'll be there in a minute, don't worry." Sam lifted himself off his stool and stretched his arms. "Well, Ronnie, thanks for the drink. And thanks for trying to look out for me, I appreciate it."

Veronica's eyes widened. "Wait, you're still going out there? Didn't you hear what I said? You're walking into a trap."

"I'm not hiding from anyone," he said. He looked at the expression of fear and confusion on her face and he smiled. "Don't be sad. Everything happens for a reason."

June picked her way around the shallow puddles that pock-marked the dirt trail that snaked through the thick woods above Cape Ernum. It had rained during the night, and the morning frost had converted some of the puddles to patches of black ice. She was running faster than usual, pushing her body to the limit, punishing her joints and lungs. Deep inside she knew she was just punishing herself. She passed an old man walking a sloppy dog, but didn't raise her head to say hello. Usually she would stop and chat, but she had other things weighing on her mind.

Earlier that morning, she had tried to convince Pete maybe they should just do Thanksgiving alone, the three of them at home, instead of joining everyone out at Oil Press island. She realized twenty-four hours wouldn't be much notice, but ever since the bridge she was scared. She didn't want anyone to think she was unthankful, especially her husband. She didn't want to be seen as a traitor.

"But Thanksgiving was your idea," he'd said an hour before, as they sat across the kitchen table from each other, drinking coffee. He pointed to the shopping bags full of food that covered all the counters and a corner of the linoleum floor. "Everyone's looking forward to it. You're roasting the turkey. The boats leave this afternoon."

"I know, I know," she said, her hands wringing the tablecloth. "I just have a bad feeling about it, that's all. You spend all your time with them now. Can't you beg out, just this once?" "I love you," he said, getting up from the table. "But I owe him everything."

"No you don't." She wanted to tell him about the van on the bridge the week before, about how she was frightened, but she didn't know how. Instead she blurted out, "You don't owe him anything."

"You're *alive*," he said, pushing up from the table. "Damn right I owe him everything." Pete picked up his weathered ballcap from the table and grabbed his jacket from the back of his chair. He looked so tired. He didn't look at her or say a word as he made his way out to the front door. She couldn't help but think that their roles had somehow been reversed; now he had the stone around his neck, but she was the one weighed down with worry.

"Well, I'm not going," she called after him, hoping that would bring him back. She could hear Stacey stirring in her bedroom upstairs, home for school break. "I'll send all the food with you, but I'm not going out there with you. Daylene will manage without me."

He shrugged. "It's a free country."

June banged the table with her open hand. "Listen, I'm scared, all right? Come back."

"I'm scared, too," he said, not turning around. He opened the door and stood there, looking outside. "But I know I have to go."

The trail came out of the woods onto pavement: she remembered Daylene's house was the last on this dead-end road, a rented double-wide with a half-inflated kiddie pool lying in the little front yard, choked with leaves. She had driven her back here once after a meeting. She hoped Daylene was home; they weren't close, but Daylene was really the only other woman she could talk to. June stretched for a moment in the street before climbing the concrete stoop and ringing the doorbell; she didn't hear anything. Behind the screen, the front door was cracked open a couple inches, so she pressed the button again and poked her head in. "Anyone home?"

Inside, she could see the place was a mess. An opened box of Froot Loops was sprawled across the shag carpet in front of the door. There was a smell of burnt glue, and the TV had an old *Designing Women* episode on, but with no sound. She was about to leave and finish her run when something stirred on the couch; she could hear a faint groan. She took another step inside. "Daylene, are you here? Hello?"

"Please tell me you're not a cop," a man's voice said. June saw a skinny scarecrow pop his head up from the couch; she'd forgotten Daylene had a brother. She'd never met Lazlo Hooker before, but she'd certainly heard about him, like everyone else around here. After all, it's hard to keep *raising the dead* a secret for long. As she picked her way through the mine-field of spilled cereal towards the sofa, she saw some tinfoil spread out on a coffee table in front of the sofa. There was a burnt-out light bulb and a Zippo there, too. She felt good about leaving the front door open, in case she needed a quick getaway. "No, I'm not a cop," she said. "My name's June. I'm a friend of Daylene?"

"Haven't seen her," he said. "She's out with Sam—you know, saving the world."

"I wanted to talk to her but I don't have her cell number, so I figured I'd just drop by."

"June," he said. "Hey, I know you. June! You're *Cancer*."

Her face suddenly felt hot. "Excuse me?"

He sat up a little. "Yeah, you're Cancer, and I'm *Drowning*. Pleased to meet you. Pretty soon we'll have a whole club of people around here, each saved from a different death by miracles. We'll have our own meetings in a secret tree house. We'll even have our own action figures. You know: *Mr. Electrocution, Mrs. Head Injury, Heart Attack Boy*. Collect the whole set! Sam Davidson will save us all!" He picked up the light bulb and held it out to her. "So you want to hit this?"

"No," she said. "Could you just tell Daylene I'm not making it to the island tomorrow?"

"I'll try to remember," he said, his eyes fluttering closed. "Can't promise anything. This white dragon is a *motherfucker*."

"White dragon?"

Now he was jerking his head around, looking at the bare walls. "Don't tell me you don't see all the dragons in here," he said, waving his hands in the air frantically. "Dragons with big dragon wings and eyes like grape jelly. Fucking *dragons*, lady."

June backed up a step. She had smoked the random joint back in high school, but this was all new territory. "Maybe I'll just leave her a note."

"Don't you see, June? You and I, we're both walking *miracles*. You'd think we'd be happier, right? You'd think we'd be living the rest of our lives on a cloud."

"Well, speak for yourself. Me, I'm thankful," she said, indignant. "Maybe you should be thankful, too. After all, you've been given a second chance at life."

"That's exactly what my sister said," he said, sitting up straight. "But no one asked *me* if I wanted to come back. I mean, would you want to come back *here*, from paradise?"

"I don't know," she said. "I never thought about it that way."

He slumped back into the saggy cushions. "That's the thing about miracles no one thinks about. Everyone automatically assumes they're a *good* thing."

She rummaged around in her jacket pockets for something to write on: a receipt, a scrap of paper or a gum wrapper, anything. Without thinking, she pulled out the business card that Sullivan guy gave her on the bridge last week, and quickly folded it in half and shoved it back in her jacket. "I'll use this take-out menu," she said, looking around quickly and spotting it on the kitchen table. "If that's okay."

"Don't see why not," he said. "Haven't eaten anything for days myself."

She found a pencil on the table and scribbled her note in the margin, then folded the paper and set it on the counter so Daylene could see it when she came in. Lazlo had picked up his lighter from the coffee table and was burning it under the bulb again, sucking out the white smoke from the end.

She wished someone else was here. "Hey, maybe you should go easy on that stuff."

"*Oui, c'est vrai,*" he said, laughing a little. "Too much might be the death of me."

She started to wheeze from the pungent smoke wafting through the room. It was time to go. She turned to leave, shaking her head as she slipped out the front door, leaving it open.

"Happy Thanksgiving, Mrs. Cancer," he called after her.

Oil Press Island sat alone like a grinded-down tooth on the edge of deep water, the northernmost island that

marked the beginning of the shipping lanes that ran east-
west across Lake Superior. It got its name from the old fish
camp there, a dozen or so plywood cabins huddled around
a smokehouse where men would live year-round, taking out
their skiffs in the dawn to drag the channel shoals, then
gutting and hanging their catch by dusk. It was the hardest
of lives. In winter when the water would freeze over, they
would walk out on the ice and drill holes for ice-fishing. In
the summer months, a boat would come out from the main-
land once a week to resupply them with wheat and tobacco
and take back boxes of smoked herring and barrels of fish
oil. The camp had been abandoned for at least fifty years,
but the shacks were still there. It made a perfect hideout,
off the beaten path.

Two boats skimmed the dark water, winding their way
around the sunken shoals of the channel, their running
lights turned off. From the pulpit of the lead boat, Judd
Sackett held onto a cleat and bounced along with the bow,
the cold spray from the waves kicking up against his gog-
gles. As the boats rounded the north end of Hermit Island,
he could see the faint outline of Oil Press up ahead.

Matty Ice kneeled beside him, checking his weapon and
slipping it back into the holster on his chest. "Still dark as
hell out here. How are we going to know who is who?"

"Sam will be the one wearing a red KISS T-shirt," Judd said.
"At least, he was wearing it when I left him, around midnight."

"That should make him easy to spot," Matty said, pressing the receiver tethered to his shoulder to relay the detail

to the rest of the team on the other boat. A voice came back to acknowledge, and Matty nodded. He leaned back against the bulkhead and closed his eyes for a second, trying to relax before they hit the island. He hooked his thumbs into his black vest. "So he's a big metal fan?"

"We both are," Judd said. "I gave him that shirt for his birthday." As they neared the island, Judd signaled the helmsman to kill the engine and switch to the trolling motor, to approach the fish camp in silence. He imagined the looks on everyone's faces when he showed up in body armor with *FBI* blazed on the front in big yellow letters. They'd probably all think he was a traitor, and the more Judd thought about it, the more he agreed with them. The only one who wouldn't be surprised would be Sam. He knew he wouldn't have the guts to look Sam in the eye when they arrested him; the only thing that made him get on this boat was the vision of that farm he had picked out, that dream of a second life that could only be a couple weeks away. He figured Sam would get some prison, maybe even a slap on the wrist; he'd be out before Judd harvested his first crop. The whole thing was political anyway, just more of the same election-year theatrics: there would be some key photo-ops of agents bringing in bad guys, and then a couple weeks later everyone would forget about it—that is, until the next time someone needed votes. All textbook. He suddenly felt sorry for Sam, and Daylene too, but he knew there was really nothing he could do now.

Matty had been watching his friend. "You two have grown pretty close, huh?"

"You could say that," Judd said, looking out at the water. He slipped his Glock 36 out of its holster and checked the breech, flipping the safety off. "You could say we were brothers."

Parable of the Good Samaritan

Winter 1983

You are sitting with your husband in the gold lounge at Charles de Gaulle, nursing a vodka tonic in a plastic glass and waiting for your flight to board. You've always liked it in here because with the sunny view and your bare feet up on an ottoman, it doesn't feel like an airport at all, except for the flat-screens that hover over the leather chairs, dispensing their constant spiral of dour international news and peppy soda commercials. You're already bored with the new crime thriller you've downloaded—how *many times can people pass a dead body in the first ten pages without noticing it?*—so once in a while you glance up at the television out of boredom.

When they show the photograph, you drop your glass to the floor.

It's a mug shot, a ghost from your distant past. Suddenly the room seems shrouded in some kind of fog. They flash her name on the screen but it's already on your tongue: *Roxy Boone*. The photo must have been taken a long time ago, because she looks exactly as you remember her, standing on that motel balcony almost thirty years ago: one tough broad. You can't hear much with the volume tuned so low, but you see the words *Capital Murder Trial—Wisconsin USA* scroll across the bottom of the screen when they show another mug shot, this one more recent, of a young man with a beard and piercing eyes.

You've seen those eyes before. You strain to read the caption below the picture: they say his name is Sam Davidson. They say he's Roxy Boone's son.

Your son.

Etienne has picked up your glass from the carpet. He's rested his hand gently on yours, but you hardly move.

So she named him *Sam*.

Etienne squeezes your hand, temporarily breaking your trance. "*Quel est le probleme?*"

You turn to him, forcing a weak smile. "Nothing, darling. I'm fine. Just tired, I guess."

The screen is showing jumpy footage, taken from the air, of a lumpy island dotted with pine trees; the scrolling caption says *Oil Press Island, Lake Superior—Three Federal Agents Killed, One Injured in Dawn Raid*. Then the screen switches to an interview with some guy in sunglasses and a dark tie; his name is Sullivan, and he's surrounded by a gaggle of reporters. The images flash too fast for you to keep up. You are trying to piece together the whole story when the screen switches again: there's a shot of an empty courtroom, then stock footage of a prison. When the new caption appears, your whole body suddenly goes numb.

Sam Davidson has been sentenced to death.

Etienne kisses your forehead. "I told you adding Stockholm to this trip was a bad idea." He gets up to stretch his legs. On any other day you'd watch him stretch with a look of longing, but right now you feel completely empty inside. "We'll be back at the house in a couple of hours. Max should already be there, no? You'll feel better when you see the boy, you always do." He smiles and takes your empty glass, heading for the bar in his striped socks. When his back is turned, you wipe away the hot tears that have started to run down your cheek. You watch him disappear into the dark fog that has suddenly filled the entire lounge like black smoke billowing from a fire.

You try to stand but your legs are numb, so you close your eyes and try to remember.

You haven't thought about that night for a long, long time.

M ost of all, you remember the bitter cold. You must have been standing next to that on-ramp to I-94 for a good hour before someone stopped. North Dakota in January was a bad place to be a girl on the run, especially when that girl only has a short skirt, a few bucks and a secondhand coat barely long enough to cover her waist.

It all comes slowly back. *Oh God*, you think: your *name*. That winter, your name was Mae West.

You remember watching the old man drive up in a dirty white pickup. He pulled up beside you on the ramp and rolled down the window; when he saw your face up close, he looked disappointed, like he expected some other girl to be standing out here freezing her ass off in the dead of a NoDak winter. He took a quick drag on his cigar and looked like he was about to drive off and leave you there, but you kind of had your foot on the bumper. "How about a ride?" you said, trying to stop your teeth from chattering.

"Where you headed, girl?"

You smiled and jerked your head west. "The ocean."

You remember his laugh, a horrible wheeze that sounded like he was throwing up, followed by a fit of coughing that looked like a seizure. Right then you promised yourself you would never, ever smoke again. You never did.

He spat out onto the pavement. "Well, better get in before you freeze to death."

Inside the truck smelled like the whole history of tobacco and sweat. There was trash on the floorboards and the patched vinyl seat felt sticky, but at least it was warm. A transistor radio stuck on the dash was playing country music. The old man rolled up his window and jerked the battered truck onto the interstate. You remember looking through the dirty back window as the truck picked up speed, watching the neon motel sign slowly shrink in the distance.

You remember taking a deep breath and mumbling to yourself, something like *anything is going to be better than what I'm leaving behind.*

The old man tells you to put on your seatbelt. "I can take you as far as Dickinson. That's where I turn off. That's two hours closer to the ocean. That good enough?"

"It's a start," you say, holding your thawing hands up to the heating vent. "Can't thank you enough for stopping, mister."

You feel his eyes on you. "You running from something?"

Two hours was going to be way too long for questions. "Why, you a cop or something?"

"Matter of fact, little lady, I am," he says. "A sheriff, actually." He pushed around the hamburger wrappers on the dashboard until he found what he was looking for: a shiny lump of metal. He held it closer so you could see in the dim light: it's a badge, all right. You can make out the words *Galilee County* crested along the bottom of the silvery star.

"Galilee's a long way," you said. It was a patent Mae West trick: someone starts asking fool questions, just ask some of your own. "Hell, mister, that's almost Montana. What are you doing down in Bismarck?"

"Had to go to the hospital. New hospital up in Galilee ain't quite finished yet."

You waved cigar smoke away from your face. "What, you sick or something?"

He started to laugh again, but stopped when it turned to another cough. "Do yourself a favor, little lady, don't get old," he said wistfully. Then he reached up to turn down the radio. "Also, I'm looking for someone. You haven't seen a guy and a girl, both about thirty, driving around in a beat-up black van? The girl especially: skinny, about thirty or so, and pleasant as a goddamn rattlesnake. You didn't see anybody like that while you were standing out there, did you?"

You knew right away he was talking about Roxy—what was her husband's name?—but you just sat there and tried your best to play it cool. "No, sir."

He shrugged his shoulders. "Worth a shot." He took another long drag on his cigar and blew a few lopsided rings into the air. "Saw your blonde hair, thought you might be the girl." Roxy had mentioned something about how she was on the run, too; she was telling the truth, all right. You feel like you're about to panic, but you know the worst thing you could do is give this guy any reason to turn this truck around.

"What's your name?" he says. "Or do I just call you Ocean Girl all the way to Dickinson?"

"It's Mae."

"Pretty name for a pretty girl."

"Thank you, sir." It wasn't your real name, but you never used your own name back then, ever since you left home. You changed it every so often like shoes or a haircut, depending on your mood. You remember spending a month in Grand Forks as Cassie Dorado, then a couple weeks in Fargo as Tiffany Case. You checked into that cheap motel in Bismarck under the name Kathy Kelley, but when you turned on the big TV in your room, you immediately got hooked on this grainy old black and white movie starring Mae West. She was *tough*. She spent the whole movie telling the dudes what to do, and you liked that. You thought the name your parents gave you didn't suit you at all. Mae West was simple, and besides, it had a direction already built in. Perfect for a girl hell bent on making it to the ocean.

You cracked the window. "What's your name? Or should I just call you sheriff?"

He thought about it for a while. "Most people just call me *El Oso*."

"That means bear in Spanish." It was the only A you ever got in three years of high school. You remember you had a crush on the teacher, Mr. Formoso, for his ponytail and the way your name slid off his tongue whenever he called attendance.

"Very good," the old man said, nodding. "Well, now that everyone at the dance has been introduced, you want something to drink? We got two hours to my exit. There's a bottle of wine under your seat there, help yourself."

"No thanks," you said. You rub your belly through your thin coat.

"Well grab it for me then," he said. "I got a long trip back home tonight."

You hesitated before reaching down and feeling a fat glass jar rolling back and forth on the floor behind your feet. When you picked it up, your nose twitched from the strong smell of alcohol, even with the lid on tight. You held it out towards him like it was a baby who needed a change. "Exactly what kind of wine is that?"

"Oh, the best kind," he said, taking it from you and resting it between his legs. "The kind that helps you forget things. Like getting out of the hospital."

You noticed the jar's barely half full. "You do a lot of drinking when you drive?"

"Got to do something," he says, unscrewing the top. "Gets lonely on the road."

You leaned away and rested your head against the door, staring at the rolling darkness outside. Once in a while you wiped away the frost in front of your eyes with your hand as your breath froze on the window. The truck rumbled under you, and your eyes got a little heavy.

"This ain't my business," he said. "But your family may be worried about you."

"I don't have a family," you snapped back. "I'm on my own."

"No family," he said slowly, in between sips. "Now *that* must be nice."

He turned up the radio again: there's a woman singing a tune called "Why Can't He Be You." She had a beefy voice, just like Mae West did when she stood on the balcony of the hotel and sang to all the cowboys in that movie. It's one of those songs you've seen old people dance to, but somehow you like it anyway. Every few minutes you can see the faint light of a farmhouse or passing car in the distance. The song is like a lullaby.

You remember waking up when the truck slowed down. You must have fallen asleep. There was an exit ramp up ahead in the darkness, but it couldn't have been Dickinson, or any other town: there were no lights, no houses, no nothing.

You stretched your arms. "Dickinson already?"

"Almost," he said. "Got to make a quick stop first."

"Here?" You peered through the frosted window, still shaking off the sleep. It's one of those countless North Dakota exits with a sign that warns NO SERVICES. "But there's nothing here."

"Only take a minute," he said. "A little business I got to take care of."

At the top of the ramp, he took a right. Suddenly you realized the truck was headed down a paved access road into total darkness. "You're scaring me," you said. You could feel your stomach lurch. "Tell me where we're going."

"It gets so lonely out here sometimes." The truck starts to shake a little; the road has turned to loose dirt. "So lonely." You can hear the gravel banging against the underbelly of the truck.

In the darkness, you could feel his hand reach between your legs.

"Stop it," you screamed, trying to get away. "*Stop* it." You reached for the door handle, but the door was locked. The truck was rolling too fast.

"I'm pregnant," you said.

"Just relax," he said, his hot breath trickling like sour milk into your ear. "I'm not going to hurt you. Why would

I do anything to hurt you? You're so beautiful." The truck slowed down and turned off the road. The headlights shone onto a farrow field, stubs of old wheat sticking out of the hardened snow. You felt his thumb brush your cheek. When his hand found the edge of your mouth, you bit down, *hard*. The old man cried out in pain. The truck slammed to a stop. You saw him cock his fist back and suddenly your whole face starburst into pain. It felt like you just ran into a brick wall. But you didn't stop struggling. His hand clamped on the back of your neck and drew you down, pinning your left arm against the seat. You reached your free hand out for something, anything. Your fingers crawled along the smooth bottom of the dashboard. You felt the keys dangle from the steering column and you grabbed onto them, pulling them out. You swung them up and connected with his face, the jagged metal digging into the old man's cheek.

"You fucking *bitch*," he yelled, letting go of your neck. You scrambled to find the door lock and suddenly you were outside, running in the frozen darkness. You could've been running in a circle for all you knew, but you didn't stop. When you realized you still had the keys in your hand, you threw them as hard as you could. The truck's headlights caught the glint of metal as they flew, and for a split second they looked like a shooting star or a drunken firefly.

You heard him groan behind you. *"Goddamn bitch, get your ass back here."*

You remember your lungs ready to explode, but you still kept on running.

Then you heard his voice in the distance, softer now. "I was just kidding—a joke, you know? Come on, we were just having some fun. Come back, okay? Come back where it's warm, Mae. Don't freeze to death out here." At some point, you realized the only reason he told you his name was because he knew you'd never live to tell this to anyone. He knew you'd take it to your grave.

When you heard the gunshot, you fell to the hard ground. The fall knocked the wind out of you, and without looking you were pretty sure your bare knees were shredded from the ice. There was another loud crack from a gun, then another. You lifted your head only enough to look across the barren field; in the shadow of the headlights, you could see him, taking a step or two in every direction like a broken toy. "*I mean it, get back here now.*" He couldn't see you, but you crawled anyway, your belly scraping against the icy ground. You felt your own blood on your lips from where he struck you. A light snow began to fall.

You'd never really prayed before, but you were willing to try.

That was when you heard the music—a trumpet?—and you remember you panicked at first, because you thought it was coming from the truck radio. But when you looked up you saw this man dressed in a suit, leaning against a sloppy stack of abandoned hay bales. It was the kind of suit with a high collar they wore in all the old movies. The man was sitting there with a brass trumpet resting on his knee, offering you a smile.

"Sure is cold out here," he said. "Reminds me of a gig I played once in Norway. Man, when you got to wipe icicles off your lips to play, you know it's cold."

"You—you've got to help me."

"Don't worry," he said, jumping up and coming over to help you to your feet. "That man's not going to find you. Not tonight, not ever. I promise you that."

"Who are you?"

"Name's Gabriel," he said, brushing the snow gently from your hair. "Some folks call me Jib. I'm sorry we had to meet like this, Mae West."

"How do you know who I am? That's not even my real name."

He shrugged. "I guess it is if you want it to be," he said, dusting some of the snow off your ripped coat. "You sure earned it. I got a few names myself. Now let's get out of here before we both freeze to death. Place gives me the creeps."

"Where are you taking me?"

He pointed his trumpet. "See that light up ahead? That's where we're headed."

You saw a prick of white in the distance. "I don't know if I can make it."

"It's not as far as you think," he said, his arm around your waist to hold you up. "Come on, Miss West. Let's get closer to that light." He started humming a tune.

You both stumbled along the lumpy ground for what felt like hours. "I can't make it," you said, about to collapse again. "Did you hear me, Jib? I said I can't go any further."

You noticed you didn't hear his humming anymore. You looked around but Gabriel was gone. The snow was coming down harder now, making it hard to see. You turned your head to see the light; you weren't moving, but the light was slowly getting closer. Soon it split in two, and you realized it was only a pair of headlights, coming towards you in the distance. You looked down at the ground and realized you were standing in the middle of the interstate. You were standing right in the middle of the road. It's almost impossible to lift your frozen arms but somehow you started to wave them above your head as the car got closer.

You opened your mouth to yell out, but no words came out.

The car slowed down to a crawl as it passed next to you. The driver's window cracked a little, enough for you to hear the two people inside. "Don't stop, Fred," a woman's voice yelled. "She looks like she's on drugs. Or in one of those cults."

The car finally came to a stop beside you. "But she really looks like she's in trouble."

"Of *course* she's in trouble, just look at her. Whacked out of her mind, probably. Don't worry, Fred, someone out here will stop," the woman pleaded. "It's just not going to be us."

"We have to help. It's freezing out there."

"Then we'll get to a phone," she said. "All you're doing is asking for trouble."

The car slowly picked up speed again, leaving you behind. You took a few steps, a crazy attempt to catch up, but that's the last thing you remember.

That was when everything turned pitch black.

You woke up in a hospital room. You knew it wasn't a dream from the soreness of your face and the throbbing from your stomach. You didn't know how long it had been since Jib led you to the highway; your body ached so much, it might have been years. You felt a stabbing pain in your gut, something different than cuts or bruises; you knew instantly that something was wrong.

After a while, a state trooper came in to ask you questions, his Smokey Bear hat slung under his arm. He couldn't understand why you wouldn't talk to him. You wouldn't say a single word. While he talked, you just stared at the light glinting off his silvery badge as if you were in a trance. When the trooper pulled up a chair next to your bed, you turned over to look out the window. The sun was starting to come up.

"At least tell me your name," he said. "Your folks might be worried about you."

"My name is Mae West."

You heard him scribble it down in his pad. "Is that your real name? Sometimes we get runaways who use an alias."

"It's real, all right," you said. "I fucking earned it."

He sighed, and you could hear him scribble some more. "I'm going to leave my card on the table here, in case your memory comes back." As the squeak of his rubber shoes disappeared down the hallway, you heard him mumble, "Come up and see me sometime."

The nurse came in with a dinner tray. She kept smiling at you while she checked your bandages and propped up your pillow.

"I lost my baby, didn't I?" you said to her.

She looked at you with that blank look of someone unsure what to say; from her face you knew it was true. But you refused to cry.

First chance you got, you escaped.

E tienne is waving his hand in front of your eyes, trying to break you out of your trance. From the concerned look on his face, it looks like he's been trying to get your attention for a while. "We should get to the gate," he says, holding up his watch. Somehow he's put your shoes back on your feet. "Are you sure everything is all right?"

Behind him, you see the same story repeat on the screen, the same images. You stare at the photo of Sam again, wondering if everything bad in his life has been your fault. The TV anchor is saying he's been found guilty of a laundry list of federal crimes. They also say he turned down any chance at appeal. He's scheduled to be put to death in some federal penitentiary back in the States.

You turn to Etienne and clutch his hand. "Do you think I'm a good person?"

He raises a bushy eyebrow as he stands up, hoisting your bag over his shoulder. "I think they mixed that last vodka tonic too strong, that's what I think." He slips his phone out of his jacket pocket to check his messages, something he always does whenever there's a conversation he doesn't want to take any further. "Okay, darling," he says with a new, cheery smile. "Last one to the gate writes the dreaded thank-you note to the Swedish Foreign Minister."

"I'm serious," you say, pulling him back down. "I need to know if I'm a good person."

Etienne puts the bag back down. He surprises you by kneeling down right in front of you. Other people in the lounge are turning to look, probably hoping they're about to witness a proposal. "I've known you for twenty years, and I can say without a doubt you are *more* than a good person," he says. "You are the best. And I love you more than anything."

You lean to kiss him. As you walk out together, you're holding onto his hand tightly. He has his arm around your waist, and it feels good. "So are you going to tell me what the trouble is now, or at thirty thousand feet?"

"Let me get my legs under me," you say. You know it will take some time; after all, suddenly you find you're a character in a whole other story, a story you forgot even existed until now. It's almost a feeling of drunkenness to be part of a completely different world, a world that has been completely buried until now. You are a woman who's been around the world, but after all this time you still feel like that girl from North Dakota, a runaway with a secret.

"Come on," he says softly, holding you tighter. "Let's go home."

The Assumption of Mary

Summer 2013

This is not a suicide note. This is what college kids call a *rough draft*—emphasis on the rough. Oh who am i kidding: this is going to be one hot mess. This is me on the forth sentence and already having no fucking clue what to write next. Its me saying fuck a lot cause it feels *good*. This isn't a cry for help. Im done crying. Its not some last will & testament either cause i've got nothing left to give. This is me ringing the bell and saying LAST CALL FOR ALCO-HOL. This is the whiskey talking; it's saying, *Roxy Boone has earned the rite to write down anything she wants.* (Ok whiskey definantly doesn't talk like that.) Whiskey would talk in a cowboy voice and spit into the campfire and say *this old bitch does not give a fuck.* This is Roxy Rebecca Boone finally learning how to use a computer because her left hand won't hold still long enough to hold a pen [fuck you DTs fuck you arthritis] This is a lonely old woman talk-

ing about herself in the third person cause she's fucking got
no one left to talk to
so fuck me
and fuck whoever invented Microsoft Word cause I have no
clue what CONTROL ALT DELETE is
and fuck Early Times cause whew! this old cow is halfway
over the moon rite now (sorry *right*)
and oh yeah while we're at it -- fuck you too, grammar
Fuck you punctuation what did you ever do for me but get
in the way? who cares about comma's and semi-colons and
conjunction fucking junction / so what if i forget a few apos-
trophys trust me there are worse things in this world to
forget / Fuck you penmanship i heard they stopped teaching
you in school now anyway / my capitol Gs always looked like
battleships / and a big fuck you to Spelling! Who cares how
words look on paper cause people just go ahead and change
the meaning anyway

ok got to admit that felt pretty good
(when i get excited on this thing i forget to hit RETURN)

But Ive got a few more phonecalls to make before I go so
why not start at the tippy-top:
Hello God?
its me Roxy   FUCK YOU   God   YEAH YOU   click
(too soon?)
i assume you're listening, you old so-and-so
i assume you know you have a problem with women right?

if you don't believe me just ask Eve & Esther & Rebecca if
they got the shaft & you turned Lot's wife into salt for turning around? I mean come on Lord
So Im dedicating this draft to the ladies / hows this for
rough:
MIZOGINIST   (the spellcheck thingy says *"misogynist"*
but I dont know, that looks weird)
well Lord, if I knew how to spell it Id tell it right to your
FACE
I bet old Ruth had the guts to say it out loud / but she didn't
write it down in her book
Or maybe after she died someone cut out all the juicy parts
where she calls you MOTHER FUCKER
ok.
i assume im going to pay for that   but i don't care
I assume anyone reading this wants to know how a woman
got so angry she called God an MFer
but you'll have to keep reading because this confession is
defiantly a Play with more than one Act
1.
Here we go, Book of Roxy chapter one: i feel like im standing in a phonebooth with a handful of dimes and a long
list of numbers to call (ok -- NOW ive got that old Jenny
Jenny song stuck in my head: *I got your number off the wall*)
but there are no phonebooths anymore which sucks -- a
whole generation will never know about making out in a
phonebooth. Will they miss how it feels to have a lover's
hot breath in your ear as you feel the phone receiver slide

up and down your back? Will they be able to tell stories if
they've never been to a bowling alley? Will they really know
love if they've never pretended to flip through Led Zeppelin
albums in the record store, making eye contact with the
cute guy on the other side of the bin? That's all gone -- so
much has slipped away from this world since i was a girl (ok
if your still reading this, right now you're thinking your girl
Roxy is slipping too. "This old bitch is *crazy*. She says she's
writing a confession but it's all about phonebooths & whiskey & goofy shit like *I* before *E* except after *G*")

                                        She goes off on all these
tangents
but that's what I'm trying to say: you live long enough, you
realize everything is a tangent / everything is another diver-
sion, even you God YEAH YOU You always like it when
the conversation comes back to you but Lord you make it
so hard for folks to find you / and you wonder why a lot of
us start drinking   so young   Lord your supposed to
be my higher power, so start acting like it: you shouldve
given me an attagirl once in a while / you shouldve bought
a round / you should've stopped taking away all the men in
my life

ok ok RETURN Roxy RETURN

God this is *tough*.
I had no idea writing things down would be such hard work.
I thought Id sit here in the living room and the words would

just leak out of my brain like ozmosis and everything I want to say would slide out in a nice neat package, like Spam or a trash compacter or when they crush junk cars into those little shiny sugarcubes. Like when they show people writing books in the movies: they look intense at the computer screen for a few seconds, bite their lip or tap their temple and then say "A HA!" before clicking away cause they've hit the motherload. Then after a fade out their tying up a stack of finished pages in string. I know that's all bullshit now -- It took me a half hour just to figure out TAB = indent on this fucking thing.

Who knew theres a difference between telling a story and writing it down? When I look at what I've written here so far I am so EMBARASSED because in real life I am smart and funny and ive been through a few of the lower rings of Hell -- but if anybody reads this they'll think I am a total joke. God Im sixty fucking years old and I've never really written anything before. Ok maybe in high school but I never got a chance to actually write a whole story down. I never got to use all those old-timey words people use when they write books -- like *hark* or *hence*. I wish I spent more time listening to Mr. Deegan read Shakespeare out loud in class and less time smoking Reds in the girls room (2nd floor by the Nurse's office) I think about all the zillion books in this world I never read and i wonder what I missed. (Like was *Moby Dick* any good? Would *Little Women* have taught me something about boys? If I read Tolstoy or Chaikovsky in high school, like the whole book cover to cover, would I

be someone different now?) I wish just once i got to be the
one to write something important, you know -- something
that starts with *once upon a time* or *it was a dark and stormy
night*. But i guess this is my last chance so
(what the Hell)
2.
It was a dark and stormy night in the little town of Nazareth. Roxy Boone sits alone in the house. She can hear the
windows rattle like a rattlesnake with the wind. She sits in
the big bed alone with a laptop computer on her lap. The
right half of the big bed is still kind of shaped like a moon
crater of Joe. Then Roxy suddenly heard a sound outside
the window. *Hark,* who goes
(ok that pretty much sucks. rattle like a rattlesnake? whoa.)
But I wont be around long enough to write a whole book
anyway. I already know there defiantly wont be a happy
ending because far as I know the ending already came and
went
hence the arsenic in my whisky glass
the Cadillac of poisons / only the best for the mother of
(you know what? fuck you motherhood: all you gave me was
an empty hole i could never fill up again) I miss Sam so
much / i miss Joe too everyday when I wake up alone in this
cold moon bed

And fuck you too Joe for leaving me all these giant plaid
shirts that still smell like you
(i know you're somewhere laughing your ass off at that, say-

ing *Oh Rock*)
I know you'll love me no matter what I say or do
that is   until I tell you what ive done to our son

When I was a girl I always thought when I get old Id be surrounded by all this evidence of a complete life, you know:
postcards and picture albums, love notes, pink sweatshirts
that say stupid shit like #1 MOM on the front. But now I
sit alone in this big empty house and I realize I have nothing. This is an old woman's prison. Every room has a different ghost, a different memory that makes me sick to my
stomach. No one ever tells you whats going to be important
when you get old, no one ever lets you in on the plan, not
even God
4.
OK Joe here it is: the hard part.
I was there when he died.
This is the part I have to get right. It was just me and Betsy
and some lawyers in this concrete room, no Daylene but I
can't blame the girl. I hear she and her brother made it to
France. We waited for hours in the little room with a glass
booth at one end, like in an old quiz show. They wheeled
Sam in on a wheelchair. They put some tubes in his arm
and left him in there, alone. I was told he couldn't here
me through the glass even if I screamed. One of them was
dressed like a doctor. There was thick glass between us but
I could hear

        God I've got to finish I HAVE TO WRITE this down

They had his arms straight out -- tied to the table in rubber straps. They had his ankles strapped down together and his neck to so he couldn't move. They told us the glass was soundproof but I swear I could hear his screams when the poison started to flow. Maybe I was just reading his lips but he kept saying "Father why?" and that's when I couldn't look anymore. I kept my head in Betsy's coat until she told me it was over. It felt like another lifetime sitting there. Someone came in and took his pulse. A guard in a uniform came in and poked him in the ribs, like he could be faking being dead. I couldn't breathe, I couldn't walk. For weeks before I got there, I told myself I would go crazy in there and rip the fucking place apart. But I just sat there until someone made me go. I don't remember where I was next, I don't remember the whole next day. I woke up here somehow, in my own bed. I used to feel like I could talk about pain, you know? I used to feel like I could even brag a little about the troubles Ive seen -- but now I know I was a complete liar because nothing weighs heavier in this world than the helpless feeling of sitting there helpless while your own son dies

Well thats one more lie Joe. There's one thing heavier: the guilt of knowing you were the one who killed him.

When im gone people will probably use my name like Benedick Arnold or that chick who broke up the Beetles. Roxy Boone, the mother who killed her own child. You know when I look at this computer screen long enough the

words starts to look different, like I didnt even write them.
But I killed my own son. I thought I could prevent his death
by telling the cops where he was but I ended up killing him
instead. I dont want him to think I was being selfish
I don't want to live in a world where they let mothers watch
their sons die
I don't want to live in a world that still puts people to Death
i dont want t talk abot it anymo r

Ok that might b the arsenic talkig but sudenly

it geting hardr to find the rite keys on this thing / i can feel
the rooms in my brain shuting down one by on / lights out
lighs ot London
          god LET ME finish this
GOD you can' kill a girl for tryng
but this is NOT a suicide note   cause tomorrows my birthday (60!!!!!!) and besides
      there's no such thng as suicide wen your already dead.
6 66
THIS iS my birthdy wish: to see my son again / to hold Sam
& Joe to / laugh lik old times
hapiness here icome n go
[haha i ass u me ths wat collge kids would call *irony*]
This s my head startng to spin / this is th room getting drak
This is m y eyes getting blury
thi is my fingrs geting num
ths is m y

tis   i
RX   Y

RE   T R   N

The Acts of the Apostles

Autumn 2013

Marseille felt like the city at the end of the world. Daylene sat outside La Samaritaine stirring her second petit noir, watching the midday crowds drift back and forth along the Quai du Port in a meandering tide. Here, it seemed like everyone was waiting; even the schoolchildren stood with their shoulders cocked. After a month watching these faces, Marseille felt like a purgatory of people on the run: artists and drifters, beggars and crooks, travelers and deserters, immigrants from hundreds of countries, revolutionaries from a dozen forgotten wars. Here, even the lovers walked like old sailors. Even the tourists shuffled past as if permanently marooned. She listened to the other tables around her, tight crushes of young men in their polished black shoes and open shirts smoking cigarettes and whispering to each other in French or Arabic or Russian, like they were all planning a jailbreak. Daylene couldn't understand much of what they were saying, but she'd learned a few things about the international language of escape. She could read it in their eyes, and in the way they cocked their heads when a stranger came too close. She was a stranger here, but it turned out Marseille was an entire city of strangers; even the locals got lost in the narrow, twisted streets of Le Panier district. When Laz brought her here, he'd told her some crazy story about Julius Caesar deciding to invade the city a couple thousand years ago. The Roman ships anchored in the harbor and found the waterfront completely deserted. Then the soldiers came ashore and marched in their straight lines into the claustrophobic maze of narrow alleys and courtyards; they vanished, a thousand men never to be heard from again.

She fixed her dark sunglasses and felt the afternoon sun on her face; she figured if a whole Roman army could get swallowed by this city shoved against the sea, a five-foot woman from North Dakota shouldn't be too much trouble.

The warm sunlight felt good on her freckled skin. She hadn't been outside for two days; that's when she was scanning the web and saw it. The story didn't take up much space on any of the news websites, but when she finally saw his mugshot and the headline—CULT LEADER EXECUTED FOR KILLINGS OF FEDERAL AGENTS—her whole body went numb.

He promised he'd come back. Right now, that was the only thing keeping her going.

Laz had bought her a spiral notebook in a corner shop and told her to start writing everything down. "Someone needs to do it," he told her. "Might as well be the one he loved the most. Sorry, sorry—*loves*. As in, present tense." It came slowly at first, mostly a lot of jumbled sentences crossed out, rewritten, then crossed out again. Random doodles. Her loopy penmanship made it look more like a little girl's diary than some kind of historical document, but that's what it was to her—a *history*—a record of what really happened. Once things started to flow, it only took her an afternoon to fill up half the notebook with memories: high school enemies, how beautiful Roxy was, her old, dear friend Jan. And Sam, of course. It felt like good therapy; she figured writing down the stories about the good times kept her mind off the bad times.

When she wasn't jotting things down, she liked to just sit invisibly and listen to all the different conversations in the cafés and on the streets. Who cared if she couldn't understand a word? It reminded her of the old story about the Tower of Babel, where God suddenly made all the people of the world speak in different tongues. When she read that story as a schoolgirl, she wondered how anything got done after that moment, before someone invented the idea of translation. How did a woman buy bread? How did a man ask someone to marry him? How did life go on? *This is what it must have felt like*, she thought; a place that thrived on confusion, an exciting city where a woman walking alone could expect catcalls in at least seven different languages.

Marseille was a city of impossible angles—the streets, the architecture, the people—but somehow life still seemed to move along at a constant rhythm. Her days here had set into their own rhythm, as well: she'd wake up in their little two-room apartment in the rundown Belsunce district and walk down the Rue des Petites Maries to the waterfront for breakfast. Sometimes she'd spend all day walking, stopping for coffee or to step into an internet café to check e-mail. At night, she would walk back to the apartment and make dinner or go down to the little blues café down the street called The Cave that somehow stocked PBR in the cooler. There was enough old American junk on the walls to remind her of home, and most nights there was live music; she'd sit in a dark corner drinking tallboys and listen to French guys on the tiny stage murder Muddy Waters or Marvin Gaye or Rick Springfield. Sometimes Laz would join her and they'd get a slow buzz until the place finally shut down for the night.

Speak of the devil, she thought: she spotted her brother coming towards her, picking his way across the stream of people from the Rue Breuteil. She noticed a wide smile on his face. "Check it out," Laz said, pulling a wad of euros halfway out of his pocket before shoving them back down. "Pay day."

Daylene sipped the last of her coffee. "You rob a bank?" It was a joke; mostly, anyway.

He sat down across from her at the little round table. "Just swung by the Western Union," he said, drumming his hands on the metal. "Martha sent us a little more fun money."

"Is that what you call it?"

"If we're having *fun* with it, yeah," he said. "But look at you, you're miserable."

"We're on the run," she said in a whisper. "We're not on vacation."

"Who says you can't do both?" He raised his arm to call the waiter over, ordering two more coffees and something to eat in his lilting French. "Listen, sister, when Lazlo Hooker goes on the run, he does it in style." He cleared his throat, folding his hands in front of him. "You know, I was thinking. Maybe you need another change of scenery. I mean, we've been here over a month. And I hear Turkey is absolutely ravishing this time of year." Daylene just stared at him with a stone face. "Okay, I *didn't* hear that, but I felt the urge to use the word *ravishing* in a sentence."

"Thanks, big brother. But this is it for me. I'm waiting right here."

"Waiting here," he said softly, tapping the table with his finger. "For him?"

"Unless you have a better idea," she said. "You're the one who sees all, knows all now, aren't you? You keep saying you can see the future. So why don't you just tell me what happens next?"

"I told you, it doesn't work like that. If I could I would, little sister. I understand how you feel."

"How? You've never been in love."

He leaned back. "What are you talking about? I fall in love at least once a week. Twice a week in the summertime."

"That's not love. You've got to be willing to give up something." She slumped into her chair, her head in her hands now. "You've got to be willing to give up everything."

They both sat there for a while, watching the different people float past La Samaritaine. Laz broke their silence. "I just don't want you to get hurt."

She let out a coarse laugh. "Then you're a little late, big brother."

"Yeah," he said, reaching for her hand. "I guess I've always been a little bit late."

Out of the corner of her eye, Daylene noticed a young guy—more of a boy, really—in a grey suit get up from a table and come over to them, grinning sheepishly. He had slicked back hair and a deep brown tan. When he started talking to her in French, she smiled politely and pointed over to her brother. They shook hands and spoke for a couple more minutes; Daylene couldn't recognize enough words to get any grasp of what they were talking about. For all she knew, Laz was selling her for a pack of menthols.

The boy turned back to her and gave a little bow. "Thank you very much, I love you," he said in his thick accent before slipping into the crowd out on the Quai du Port. Laz didn't say anything; he just took out his pack of smokes from his shirt pocket, shaking one out into his mouth. Then he lit it, taking his time rolling smoke in and out of his lungs.

"Well? What did he want?"

"Honestly? He thinks you're pretty. Wanted to know if you'd like to grab a drink sometime." He took another drag, turning to watch the stream of people passing by. "He's got a thing for American girls, which is a damned shame, because he's just my type. Damn, don't you love a country where men get up and come over to your table?"

Daylene reached over and grabbed his arm. "Okay, and what did you say?"

He turned to her and smiled. "I told him, this girl here is *taken*," he said, kicking his feet up on an empty chair. "I told him, she's waiting for a guy who should be back any minute."

One minute, Pete was sitting in the back of the transfer bus next to his cellmate, a teenage blabbermouth who called himself Lil' Dookie, listening to him brag about how easy it was to steal money from cash machines these days. "Computers," Dookie said, banging his manacles against the metal rail on the seat in front of them like he was drumming along to music. "I mean, *passwords*? Give me a break. Encryption, my ass. It's all mathematics, am I right?" He was shouting over the loud chug of the diesel. The rest of the bus was empty except for a sleepy CO driving and a tall guy in a suit riding shotgun, up front in the cage. Pete recognized the guy in the suit from the courtroom; some kind of federal agent. Dookie leaned forward to rub his runny nose against his forearm. There was a black tattoo on the back of his hand that was either a really good Abraham Lincoln or a really bad Cher. He nudged Pete with his bony elbow. "So, old man—what did they get you for, anyway?"

The next minute, there was a blinding flash of light and the world went blank.

When he came to, Pete was up to his waist in a muddy creek; he could feel his bare feet rubbing against the smooth rocks on the bottom. Somehow his legs and hands were free. The water was cold enough to chill his legs to the bone. He slowly opened his eyes and saw it was dark out, but soon realized he was just looking up at the dark underbelly of a bridge.

He could hear a voice—no, two voices—moaning in the distance. He reached down into the mud to pull his legs out of the water, but his head throbbed when he tried to move, like someone was taking a hammer to his skull.

"Easy, old man." It was the kid, Dookie, sitting on the creek bank next to him. "We had one hell of a crash."

Pete could remember looking out the grimy window of the prison bus, minding his own business; he recalled watching the thick woods slip by, the leaves on the trees already turning red and brown. Once in a while the trees would disappear and there would be a field or a fence, a house or a shed. Then another wall of trees. He could remember slipping into a daydream where he was holding June's hand as they walked through the woods behind their house, back in Cape Ernum. But daydreams were the only kind of dreams he could afford these days; at night after lights out, he'd lie on his rack in his cell for hours, unable to sleep. When he did there were only nightmares, the same vision of that morning on Oil Press Island. He was haunted by it: how he let down Sam that night, how he showed everyone just what a coward he really was. They had given him six years in the pen for shooting that federal agent's ear off on Oil Press Island. *Some revolutionary I turned out to be*, Pete thought. *I can't even shoot straight.* Right now, prison didn't seem like much punishment compared to how he felt inside. His lawyer had been almost giddy when the judge finished talking at the sentencing hearing. "Six years," the lawyer had said to him, already hugging his shoulders. "You'll be out in three. Happy day."

June had hugged him quickly, too, and told him the news: Sam had been put to death at midnight last night. Lethal injection. Sam didn't file an appeal; didn't want one. *Happy day*, Pete echoed in a voice that barely reached a whisper. He'd got three years in jail for shooting some poor guy's ear off. Sam was already dead even though he didn't strike a soul.

What a rotten world, he thought: rotten and unfair and hopelessly broken.

He could remember the back end of the bus rattling like a box of nails every time it hit a bump on the old country road. Dookie had been nudging his arm again. "So what *did* you do, fella? You can tell me, I can take it."

Pete slumped back in the seat, his eyes still out the window. "I was a fisherman."

Dookie bucked like he was riding a horse. "You see? That's what I'm *talking* about here. Can't even catch a fucking fish these days without these clowns calling it a crime. Am I right?" His paper slippers were tapping furiously against the floor, like he was practicing a dance routine at triple speed. At that moment, Pete remembered thinking any penance he was going to get in the Sour Hereafter might be better than having to sit there and listen to this cocky kid drone on for eternity. If there was a Hell, it probably had Lil' Dookie working the door. "Hell of a country, am I right?"

Pete could remember thinking *Please, Please Shut the Hell Up* but saying instead, "Hell of a country." And then he could remember the CO at the head of the bus finally waking up long enough to bang the butt of his shotgun against the mesh, telling them both to shut the hell up.

That was the exact moment when the whole world went bleach white.

Daylene hunched over her notebook in her usual booth at The Cave while the owner, a wide Algerian man named Baz, came out from behind the bar every so often to bring her a fresh beer. He took his time because there was really nothing else for him to do; even for a Tuesday, the place was dead. When there was music, young bohemian types packed the old walnut bar and half-dozen tables and drank the house sangria, but Baz had mentioned his regular band canceled at the last minute; now the whole week was ruined. He leaned on the bar and looked out on the empty street; every time he saw someone pass the glass door, he sighed. "When there is no music, there is no drinking. When there is no drinking, there is no money."

"What are you talking about, Baz? This is my third beer," she said, holding up her glass.

He rolled his big eyes. "Yes, my friend," he bellowed. "With your help I am ready to buy the plane to bring my wife and children over from the *Qasbah*." He slid open the well cooler and reached down to pull out a fresh can of PBR. "I have found *une remplacante* to play music, but he will not be here until tomorrow."

"So you managed to get Phil Collins after all?" She knew two things about Baz Anwar: one, every Monday morning he would wire money back to his family in Algiers. And two, if there was a Church of Phil Collins, Baz would be the high priest.

"Do not joke about Phil Collins," he said, swooning as soon as she mentioned the name. He kept his eyes closed for a good minute, as if trying to recover his strength. "No, this man is American, like you. I can tell from his accent on the telephone." He stood there, teetering on the balls of his feet with his hands behind his back, peeking over her shoulder at the notebook. "Are you writing a novel?"

"Not really," she said, trying to cover more of it with her hand. "More like a history, or a memoir. But there's a story in here somewhere, that's for sure."

He shook his head. "I like novels. My favorite is—how do you say—crime thriller?"

"Murder mystery," she said, nodding. "Whodunits. Some folks call them *potboilers*."

He tilted his round head and pointed down at the page. "So this book is not potboilers?"

She hadn't thought about this amounting to an actual *book*; she hadn't thought about the possibility of someone else reading it, either. "Well, someone gets killed," she said; thinking about Sam made her stop and take a deep breath. "But by the end, you kind of already know why. I mean, it's not much of a surprise."

He made a face like he'd bit down on a lemon. "I do not think I would enjoy that."

"Yeah, well," she said, holding up her glass in a toast. "Join the club."

He was still hovering over her. "Does it have the sexy parts, at least? Like *un roman d'amour*? You know," he said as he began to move his hips in a slow circle, his arms straight out. Daylene covered her eyes as if she were witnessing a twelve-car pileup on the freeway, making him laugh. "Why are you afraid? This is my dance of sexy," he said, still gyrating. Daylene wouldn't say this out loud—he was a nice guy—but she couldn't help noticing the Dance of Sexy looked a lot like a fat man working a hula hoop.

Or maybe Elvis trying to find a toilet in the dark.

Luckily, she heard the door jingle open behind them. "You've got customers, Baz."

"You should put me in your story," he said, strolling back towards the bar. He was already breathing hard from the workout. A man wearing a seersucker suit hesitated in the doorway, unsure of what he was walking into. He had polished wingtip shoes that glowed in the dim light, and a fat-brimmed hat Daylene had only seen in old movies. She noticed the black case hanging from his hand; from its shape she guessed it held a trumpet.

Baz looked the stranger over for a moment, then waved him over to the bar with a friendly paw. "I think every story should have dancing in it, *d'accord?*"

The man pushed back his hat and scratched at his temple. "Was that dancing?"

"Hot damn," the kid said. "Never been part of a real live Act of God before."

Pete rubbed his head. "What the hell happened?"

Dookie threw his arms up. "Don't really know. I woke up a few minutes ago, up there on the bridge with my cuffs off. The two bulls are still up there, both out cold. Breathing, though, like they're asleep. As in, not *dead*. The bus is still up there, too, and it ain't crashed, either, just stopped in the middle of the fucking road like it's waiting for a light to change. When I crawled down here and found you, damned if you didn't have no cuffs on, either. They're just *gone*, as in disappeared. You see what I'm saying, old man? I'm telling you, it's an Act of God all right. Somebody upstairs wants

Lil' Dookie out of jail, and *fast*. Swear to God I'm going to start praying and going to church and helping old ladies cross the fucking street and—"

"You're babbling, son," Pete said, dragging himself up on a flat rock. He was still trying to catch his breath. "And stop calling me old man. My name's Pete Romack. Wait—you *crawled* down here, you said? Are you hurt?"

"Hot *damn*," Dookie said again, his head floating somewhere in the stratosphere.

Pete sat up and gave him a closer look; from the wild look in his eyes the boy was either in shock, or having the time of his life. Maybe both. "I said, are you hurt?"

"Hot damn, I can't believe I'm in a real, live, honest-to-God *jailbreak*." The kid's eyes kept darting around. "Only thing would make this better is if there was a one-armed man I had to hunt down—you know, for revenge," he said. "Just like Harrison Ford."

Pete managed to crack a smile; this kid was a goofball, all right, but a goofball that was growing on him. He kind of reminded him of his little brother: twenty percent smart ass, eighty percent mouth. "So you like old movies?"

"If they got a jailbreak in it, I do." Dookie rubbed his dirty forearm against his nose, leaving a jagged streak of wet mud across his face, a slash of black war paint. "By the way, I think my leg's broke."

Pete thought the boy was kidding until he saw the pained, desperate look in his eyes. He looked down at the bottom of Dookie's muddy jumpsuit; sure enough, one of his legs was crooked like a shillelagh below the knee. Dark red blood was already drying on his bare foot. All the confusing chatter made sense now: the boy *was* in shock. "Okay," Pete said, sliding closer. "Let me take a look at that."

"Whoa, hold on—what are you gonna do, scale me? You said you were a fisherman."

"I lied," Pete said, trying to keep a calm voice. "I'm really a doctor. Like Harrison Ford."

The kid eyed him suspiciously. "No shit?"

"No shit." Pete sat up all the way. "What's your real name?"

"Why the hell you want to know that?"

"Because if I've got to say 'Little Dookie' out loud one more time, I'm going to kill myself, all right?"

"It's Marc," the boy grumbled, as if giving up his secret identity. "Marcus DuFresne."

"Nice to meet you, Marcus. Now," Pete said. "Let me look at that leg of yours."

"Hot *damn*," the kid said again, fidgeting like crazy. "If you're a doctor then you got to find the nearest hospital and steal some janitor dude's ID. Then you got to dye your hair black. Then you call—no, don't call any of your old friends, especially the old dude who lives in the basement. Then you go to Chicago and find that fucking asshole." He was getting even more erratic; pretty soon he might pass out from the shock.

"Which asshole is that?" Pete worked his hands on Marc's leg. The skin there felt cold.

"What do you mean, *which asshole is that*? The one-armed man," he said. "Keep up."

Pete didn't answer right away; he closed his eyes and whispered a short prayer, like Sam had taught him. Their days on the island seemed like a long time ago.

"Whoa, I can move it now," Marcus said, amazed. "That's some Mr. Miyagi shit right there. How the hell did you do that?"

"Trust me," Pete said, helping him to his feet. "You don't want to know."

"Just answer me one question," Marc said. "And no bullshit, okay?"

"No bullshit."

He pressed a finger into Pete's chest. "Hey, are you some kind of angel?"

"No," Pete said. "Whatever the opposite of an angel is, I'm that."

The boy was following behind him. "So you're a devil."

"Yeah, a devil. Now are you ready for your honest-to-God jailbreak?"

"I can come with you?" The boy was running in place. "Hot damn, hot damn."

"Son, what the hell were you in prison for?" For a kid who liked to talk like a gangster, Pete thought he seemed pretty harmless.

Marc shrugged. "Stole a car."

"That's not so bad."

"Police car."

Pete nodded. "Then you might turn out to be useful after all." The kid was right about one thing: this was an Act of

God. After all, Pete knew from first-hand experience. Maybe someone up there still thought they could use an old fisherman. Maybe someone thought Pete Romack deserved a second chance at keeping promises.

There was only one way to find out.

The horn player said some people called him Jib. "Other folks call me Gabe," he said, stepping up on the little stage and unpacking his trumpet from its old leather case. "Depending on the gig, some folks've called me a lot worse." He smiled bashfully. "But y'all don't strike me as the egg and tomato-throwing type." When he took off his hat and hung it on one of the microphone stands on the stage, Daylene noticed he was a lot younger than he first appeared; maybe it was the vintage clothes, the shaved head, or his deep voice. But now she could see his smooth, unwrinkled skin and bright eyes and she guessed he couldn't be more than college age.

"You do not have a band?" Baz said, looking towards the door as if more people were about to come in. "You are alone?"

"Just me," Jib said, smiling. "A regular one-man band."

Baz furrowed his bushy eyebrows and slid into the booth beside Daylene while the trumpet player got ready on stage. Baz sat there restlessly and rubbed his chin, nudging Daylene's arm. "He is very young," he said in a low voice. "Do you think he knows the songs of Phil Collins?"

"Come on, Baz," she whispered back. "He might be a little young to remember that."

Somehow from the other side of the long room, the young man had heard them. "I know I don't show it, but I'm older than I look." Baz and Daylene looked at each other, wondering how he could have listened so closely from that far away.

She shrugged. "He's got good hearing, at least."

The musician pursed his lips and blew a few long, sad notes. He sat on a stool with one leg up, the trumpet pointing down into the floor like he was playing for the mice in the basement. Daylene wasn't anywhere near an expert in jazz or blues, but right away she could tell this guy was *good*. The notes slipped out like a slow drip of oil. After a few minutes, he rolled his neck and launched into something a lot faster, a lot more upbeat. Daylene knew the tune, but she couldn't pinpoint the name of it right away.

When she looked over at Baz, he was already on his feet and clapping. Then the old song came to her: it was Phil Collins, all right. *Su-su-sudio.* He looked like he was about to do the Dance of Sexy again, so she grabbed his thick arm and pulled him back down to the table.

Jib played a few more old melodies. When he started into an old Algerian folksong that Baz had only heard as a child, the club owner got up from the booth and started clapping again. "Enough, enough," Baz said. "You are hired."

Jib flashed a wide smile. "Thank you kindly." He unscrewed the mouthpiece to his horn, then took a white handkerchief from his pocket and started to rub down the brass.

Baz stepped closer to the stage. "I am glad you came a day early, my friend."

Jib nodded. "Thought I'd come by early for an audition, show you what I got. Besides, I heard there was another Yankee hanging around in here," he said, looking over at Daylene. "You don't run into to a lot of folks from North Dakota in these parts."

"This is true," Baz said, raising a finger in the air. "In Paris, you see so many Americans. But in Marseille, you only see Americans who are running from something. Or lost."

Suddenly Daylene felt a jagged bolt of paranoia edge up her spine. Now she was standing up, too. "Wait," she said. "How did you know I used to live in North Dakota?"

"We know some of the same people," he said in a low voice. "Sam, especially."

She folded her arms across her chest. "You know Sam." Suddenly her skin felt hot.

"Yes ma'am," he said. "We're old friends."

"Funny, I've known him since high school, and I've never once met you, mister."

He let out a little laugh. "Older than that." Jib finished putting his trumpet away and wiped his forehead with the handkerchief before stuffing it back in his pocket. "Can we talk?"

"Depends on what you want to talk about."

"I have a message for you," he said, stepping down from the stage. "From Sam."

"Bullshit," she said. "If Sam wanted to see me, he'd come himself."

Baz glanced back and forth between them, not quite sure what was going on. "Old friends coming together in my establishment," he said, throwing his arms up in the air. He turned and headed for the bar with a full head of steam. "This calls for drinks on the house."

"No thanks, Baz," Daylene said, still glaring at the stranger. "This certainly ain't no friend of mine."

"Even if I told you Sam was alive?"

"Where is he?"

"Not too far from here," he said, sitting down across from her. "You got a good pair of walking shoes, maybe even a backpack? It's gonna be a good stretch of the legs, that's for sure."

"I got shoes. Don't have a backpack, though."

"I think your brother Laz has one. Look under his bed tonight."

She leaned closer over the table, still deciding whether to trust this guy, or to slug him. "Let me ask you: how do you know all this?"

"I told you," he said. "I'm older than I look."

Pete could hear a helicopter droning somewhere in the distance.

"So tell me," the kid said to him. "Who the hell is Kris Kristofferson?"

Pete stopped and turned around. "What kind of question is that?"

"You were talking to yourself again," Marc said. "You were kind of singing, too."

"Really? What did I say?"

"You said, *maybe Kris Kristofferson was right.* Then you said, *freedom's another word for nothing left to lose.* You sang that last part."

"Sorry," he said. "It's an old song. He's an old singer."

"Old, like 'N Sync?"

Pete shook his head. "Older than that."

"And don't be sorry. It's kind of cool when old folks dream out loud."

"For the last time, I'm *not* old."

"Well, how old are you?"

"Turned forty-one last week."

Marc whistled like a bomb dropping. "Yeah, you're old." He hopped over a fallen log, a kid on a nature walk. "So for the last time, what did you do? You catch an illegal whale or something?"

"I shot a guy in the ear."

"*Sick.*" The boy stopped for a moment. "Was it an accident?"

"I was aiming for his chest," Pete said. "I thought I was saving a friend."

"You don't seem like the kind of guy who uses guns a whole lot."

"Yeah, well, I guess that's why I hit him in the ear."

The trees started to thin out and the two men found themselves on the edge of a clearing behind what looked like a deserted warehouse. Pete crouched down behind a rock and pulled the kid down next to him. "Here's where you earn your keep, son." He pointed across the clearing to a black Durango parked next to a rusty stack of metal pipe. "Tires look good. Think you can start that up?"

"Are you kidding? In my sleep." Marc rubbed his chin. "Where we headed?"

"Home," Pete said. "We're going home."

The Rue du Camas wound past the northern slums of the city, mazes of big cinder-block apartment buildings with laundry lines drooping from the balconies. She had felt sick to her stomach that morning. Luckily, Jib was walking ahead of her slowly; every so often he'd stop and look around. "Slow and steady wins the race," he said, wiping his forehead under his hat.

"You still haven't told me where we're going," she said with a sigh. "Or how far."

"Hey, we're artists, you and me," he said. "Artists walk."

She laughed. "You mean, *you're* an artist."

"You're a writer, aren't you? I saw you writing that book."

"That's not art," she said. "That's just something to keep me sane."

"Sounds like the same thing to me."

By noon they had reached the rocky outskirts of Marseille. Ahead, she could see the start of green hills and a massive, rolling cemetery coming up on their left. "War dead," Jib said solemnly. "Battle of Marseille, back in World War II. Leveled half the city."

"Did you see it?"

"I did," he said. "Bloody as hell, far as battles go."

"I don't understand," she said. "You just let it happen? If you were here, why couldn't you do something about it? I mean, you're an angel, aren't you?"

He stopped to wipe his brow. "All I can say is, don't shoot the messenger."

"It just doesn't make sense to me. None of it does." She spat on the pavement, trying to get rid of the stale taste in her mouth. "And if you say *have a little faith* one more time, I'm going to punch you right in the eye, got it?"

"Got it," he said.

Suddenly a voice boomed loudly from behind the cemetery wall. "Hey, stranger," it said. She knew before turning around that it was Sam. She didn't say anything, she didn't even move at first. She just wanted to hold him.

"You can't touch me," he said, backing away like he was dodging hornets. "Not yet."

"So you're not really here," she said, pulling back. "You're like a ghost." She shook her head. "Story of my life."

She could see the sadness in his face. "Listen, I know you've come a long way," he said. "You just need to go a little further."

"Then why are you here at all?"

"I wanted to see you," he said. "I needed to see you."

There was a bag of dirty laundry stuffed in the backseat, so Pete rummaged through to find something they could both wear while Marc slowly pulled the Durango out of the lot and onto the road. "Don't give me anything polyester," the boy said. "Makes my skin break out."

"Not a lot of choices," Pete said, pulling a couple shirts and pants out.

"I found a twenty in the cupholder," Marc said. "I sure am hungry."

The sun was going down, but up ahead Pete could see an old country cemetery looming in the distance. "Do me a favor, pull up over there."

"Are you kidding? This is a jailbreak, old man. Not a sightseeing tour."

"Just do it, okay? Trust me." He slipped a striped shirt over his head.

Marc rolled the black truck off the side of the road and next to the cemetery wall. Pete got out and looked up and down the empty road. "Be right back."

"This is crazy," Marc said.

Pete closed the door and ran around the front of the truck, taking the wall with a tired leap. From the truck, Marc watched him pick his way through the stones, like he was looking for something. Marc started to panic, putting his hand on the gear shift at least a dozen times. Finally, he could see Pete coming back. It looked like the old man was actually *smiling.* Pete jumped back over the fence and got into the truck. "Let's roll," he wheezed, out of breath.

"I was about to give up and leave your ass here," Marc said. "What were you doing?"

Pete slapped the boy's shoulder. "Visiting a friend."

There was a farmhouse at the end of the road. In the moonlight, Daylene could make out an old stone barn looming on their right, its rooster weathervane squeaking gently with every gust of wind. Ahead, the road they had been following all night narrowed into a gravel track until it finally ended in a wire fence; behind that, a field of tall grass. "Great," she said, turning to Jib. "What now?" They had passed the last crossroads hours ago.

"We're almost there," he said, wiping his brow. "At least it's a beautiful night."

"If my feet didn't ache so much, I'd stop and look at all the stars. But—" Just then, Daylene froze; she could hear something moving towards them in the field. She turned to see black figures moving towards them in the dim light. But after a moment she realized it was only a few curious goats, coming closer to investigate. The little bells on their necks rang softly as they stuck their necks through the wire. "Goats," she said.

Jib walked over to the open barn door and peered inside. "Hello?" No answer. "Looks empty enough. Guess we should get some sleep. Big day tomorrow."

"What, *here*?" She stuck her nose inside. The barn smelled like a hundred years of goats.

"Sure," he said, already sitting down on a fat pile of straw. "Unless you see a Super 8 down the street or something." He began to untie his shoes. Daylene hadn't budged from the doorway. After a while, he looked up at her and smiled, jerking his thumb towards the back corner behind him. "Come on, I found you a nice patch over there. They call it the executive suite. Besides, they say you haven't lived until you spend the night in a French barn."

"Who says that?"

"You kidding?" He pushed down the straw next to him like he was testing a mattress. "Tourists spend a lot of money for rustic accommodations like this."

"It's rustic all right." But she was too tired to argue. Even her neck and shoulders throbbed from carrying the backpack all day. She crawled behind him into the stack of hay bales in the corner. When she leaned back, her eyes already felt heavy; she didn't even want to know how much straw she had in her hair. "Hey, Jib," she said with a yawn, barely able to get the words out.

"Yeah, darlin'?" He had been humming a tune under his breath.

"Tell me all this bullshit is worth it," she mumbled, slowly drifting off to sleep. "Promise me everything's going to turn out all right. Promise me when I wake up it's going to be all guns and roses from now on."

"Okay," Jib said, laughing and scratching his scalp. "When you wake up, it's going to be all guns and roses from now on."

"*Mmmmmmm*, roses," she moaned, already halfway into a dream. "Thanks."

When Daylene woke up again, she had to shield her face from the bright morning sun filtering down through the cracks in the crooked rafters. She spit out a piece of hay from her lip. "Rustic," she laughed to herself. "Someone ring for the maid."

"*Allo?*" There was a strange voice coming from the barn door, a young man's voice, maybe a boy. "*Qui est la?*"

She turned over and whispered to Jib. "Hey, angel, how do you say *don't shoot* in French?" With any luck, this guy loved Phil Collins, too. Jib didn't say anything, so she turned to him; he wasn't there. He was gone. In a way, she wasn't surprised; after all, that was the story of her entire life, men she cared about coming and going.

Great, she muttered under her breath. *Alone again.* "Don't shoot," she said.

"But this is not a gun," he said. "It is a broom."

A woman's voice called from the farmhouse. "Max? *Toute est bien?*"

"*Oui, maman*," he yelled back. "But I think we have a visitor."

Daylene shook the straw from her hair and followed the young man outside. She squinted in the new sunlight. A pretty woman in jeans and a barn coat was coming towards them from the house. "*Bienvenue*," she said, extending her hand. "*Vous etes perdu?*"

Daylene's French was good enough to understand. "Not lost, really. Just a wild goose chase, I guess."

"You are American," the woman said. "We don't get much visitors out here on the farm, especially ones from the States." She spoke English like she was from the Midwest, maybe even North Dakota. "Why don't you join us in a little breakfast? I just set some out on the patio."

"Thanks, but—" Daylene said, looking around the place. "I was with someone, but I guess he ducked out on me." She turned to Max. "You didn't see a guy in a funky suit and wingtips around here at all, did you?"

"I believe I would have remembered that." Max shook his head. "I am hungry, *maman*."

Suddenly, the woman's face went pale. "Max, you really should finish all your work before you sit down to eat."

"*Mais*—"

"Don't argue," she said. "I'm still your mother."

Max slapped his gloves against his leg and trudged back towards the barn.

The woman stood there, frozen.

"Are you all right?" Daylene said to her. "You look like you saw a ghost or something."

She waited for her son to disappear into the barn. "My name's Mae. It used to be, anyway." She turned and headed back towards the house, beckoning Daylene to follow her.

As promised, there was a spread of bread, cheese and fruit on a table behind the house. "Wingtips, you said? And did he have a trumpet or a horn with him?"

Daylene had forgotten how hungry she was; out of instinct, she reached for the food. "That's the guy," Daylene said, her mouth already half-full of bread. "You saw him?"

Mae slumped back into her chair. "A long time ago." As Daylene ate, Mae studied her, wincing every so often. "I'm sorry, but I need to ask you one more question. Are you pregnant?"

Daylene almost choked. "What the hell kind of question is that?"After she swallowed what she had in her mouth, she took a deep breath and tilted her head to the side. "How could you tell?"

Mae took a sip of her coffee. "Call it an educated guess."

"Guess I need to stop smoking for real, then," she said. "Bad for the baby and all."

Mae's face slid into a tired smile as she let out a long sigh, like she'd been through this same conversation before. "Live a little."

Daylene could hear someone clear his throat behind her, and when she turned there was a man in pajamas and bare feet standing in the doorway, leaning his arm on the frame and scratching at his curly salt-and-pepper locks. He was wearing a wrinkled white T-shirt that was at least a few inches short for his pale snowdrift of a belly. His eyes were still half-closed from sleep. "*Bon matin,*" he said, yawning. He looked over at Daylene. "*On a de la visite?*"

"Etienne, this is Daylene. She's an old friend of mine from North Dakota." Mae ran her finger along the edge of the table. "I think she might be staying with us a while."

He raised an eyebrow, letting the news settle. He rubbed his eyes and glanced over at the two cars in front of the house. "Did she walk from North Dakota?"

"*Mon chou*," Mae hissed at him. "She is our guest."

His frown melted away into an easy smile. "I am sorry. Welcome to our home. I ask too many questions, a bad habit to acquire when you work for the government so long." He stood there with a stooped back, pawing at his protruding belly. "Has my wife told you I am also an excellent cook?"

"Oh, she sure did. That's why I'm here, actually," Daylene said, sharing a conspiratorial glance with Mae from across the table. "I heard about the crepes."

He straightened up a bit, happy with the compliment. "Breakfast will be ready—how do they say in America?—in two shakes of a sheep's tail."

"Lamb," Mae said, chuckling a little. "It's lamb, baby."

"*Zut alors, l'agneau. Pas de mouton. D'accord.*" He bowed slightly to his new guest and shuffled back inside the house. The two women could hear him in the kitchen, whistling a tune to himself as he moved around. After a few moments, they could hear metal pots banging together, then crashing to the floor.

Mae was still laughing. "If I know my husband, he'll be in that kitchen for the next four or five hours. Enough time for you to tell me *everything*." She took a sip of her drink and settled deeper into the chair. "Don't leave anything out."

Daylene had no idea where to start. She looked around for her backpack, hoping something in her notebook could spark her memory. She pulled out the tattered mess of pages and flipped through a few, but now there was a weird feeling settling into the pit of her stomach, different than a baby. She realized it was only weird because she'd never really had it before; it was that warm feeling of belonging, an easy sensation of slow motion that Daylene didn't even know existed until this very moment. When soldiers returned from war, they longed for that feeling of returning to normal, and if she thought about it, she'd been through war too; she'd spent the entire first half of her life having to run away or disappear. She was used to dodging the rest of the world, only stopping in one place long enough to catch her breath. Daylene realized this place felt weird to her because it felt *right*. It would take a little getting used to. She took a gulp of coffee, hoping it would break up whatever was blocking her throat, choking her. Then a word came to her lips, a word she'd never really said out loud before: *home*.

"You know you can stay here as long as you want," Mae said, leaning over and patting her knee. "Now, come on. Give me the whole story."

Daylene's mouth opened and closed a few times, unsure of what to say. "God, the whole story," she said. Suddenly she was out of breath, daunted by all the details. "Where do I start?"

"I want you to start at the beginning," Mae said. "I want you to tell me everything."

Second Epistle of Paul to the Romans

Autumn 2013

To: Poncho S. Pelotti, Acting Commissioner <ppelotti@ irs.gov>

From: Patrick Sullivan, Special Agent IRS-CI <psulliva3@ irs.gov>

cc:

Re: Re: Re: Re: Progress Report?

Hi Punchy:

This is going to be the strangest letter of resignation you're ever going to get.

Right now you're sitting at your desk drinking your instant coffee out of that #1 DAD mug and when you read this, you're checking the calendar to make sure it's not April Fools day or your birthday. But this is no joke. I've even changed my name. By the time you read this, it'll be Monday morning and I won't be Pat Sullivan anymore. I'll be a new man and I'll be long gone, completely off the grid.

Honestly, I'm surprised the phone still works.

I can't give you a real explanation; I don't even know the whole story myself, and besides, I don't have a lot of time. I am on the run. This is what I remember: I was catching a ride on the prison transfer bus, baby-sitting one of the Sicarii affiliates we nailed to the wall, when everything goes white, like a flash of lightning in my face. When I woke up, I can feel I'm lying on the road but I couldn't see anything, it's like I was snowblind. I thought, I am dreaming. Then there was this deep voice like a tuba calling my name. To be honest, now that I think of it, the voice kind of sounded a lot like James Earl Jones. "Sully," the voice says to me. "Why are you chasing me?"

I yell out but there's no answer.

Someone found me there on the side of the road. Three days later, when my sight slowly came back, I found myself in the backwoods shack. I would mention names but they're on the run, now, too. Who saves me, Punch, but the same people I've spent a whole career trying to stomp out? You guessed it: the zombie roaches. I realized I've become the very thing I hate. I realized I've spent a whole life learning to be a hunter when I was supposed to be the hunted. Until now, I could never tell you what irony is, even if my life depended on it; I always thought it was just a word college kids had to learn to sound smart, then forget.

Something *happened* to me, Punch. I can't tell you what, I can't even tell you my new name, since it'd make it that much easier for you guys to find me. I woke up to a new world, one where the old rules don't matter so much. I always thought I was a hero, you know, righting wrongs, catching the bad guys, leaping embezzlers in a single bound. Now I see there are no heroes in this world. This world doesn't need heroes anymore.

So here's to irony: I guess now I'm one of the roaches. Which means I'm getting used to a life on the run. But a while ago, I read somewhere that a billion years from now, when we're all dead and gone, the roaches will still be here.

Adios, my friend, and Vaya con Dios.

Hugs & Kisses (for real this time)
Not Sully

> *(sent from my iPhone)*

Epilogue: The Cave of Hira

Mamadou let out a long sigh as he opened the cash register to re-count the money they'd taken in that morning, the same money his uncle said he'd just counted a minute ago. The little corner shop had only been open a half-hour but Talib had written down an impossible number—$135,000—on the notepad; by that count, they should be multi-millionaires before lunchtime. It only took a quick inspection of the till for Mamadou to shake his head in disgust and look around the counter for a pencil. He crossed out the number his uncle had scrawled and replaced it with $13.50. The old man couldn't count, but he definitely could cook; if Little Senegal was its own tiny country here in southeast Phoenix, wedged into the four square blocks between the Baseline and Superstition Freeway in the neighborhood locals called Bekka, then everyone agreed that Abu Talib's kerosene double-burner stove must be the unofficial capital.

The sign outside had fallen down years ago from neglect and rust but luckily, the heavenly aroma of Talib's *bassi-salte* wafting down Minton Street was more than enough advertising.

Mamadou heard the door buzzer and looked up to see a couple of teenagers saunter in, a blast of hot air and sunlight coming with them from outside. He'd seen them before. "Eighteen years old for cigarettes," he said sternly, already pointing to the warning sign above the counter. They immediately swiveled and went back out into the heat again, grumbling under their breath.

Talib came out from the back, wiping his huge gnarled hands on an apron that stretched over his belly, a small constellation of tomato paste splattered across it. "Cowboys," the old man said, scratching at the short-cropped hair under his knit cap. "All they want is beer and cigarettes, beer and cigarettes. And dirty magazines."

"We don't sell dirty magazines," Mamadou reminded him, not looking up.

"Well, if we did," he said, raising a finger in the air. "The cowboys would want them."

The old man called anyone in this city with fair skin a *cowboy*. He'd come to Arizona more than twenty years ago—a member of Senegal's old ruling class exiled after the failed Dia coup—and even now, the old man still half-expected to see John Wayne riding shotgun on a stagecoach down Kyrene Road when he walked home from the shop at night. Such must have been the power of the one movie house in Dakar back in the 60s, Mamadou thought.

He pointed to the notepad next to the register. "You counted wrong again."

"The computer counted wrong," Talib said, folding his arms. "Besides, we are *artists,* are we not? We have no need for money." Mamadou felt another argument brewing like a sudden dust storm, so he pushed himself up to stand straight when the door buzzed again; he could smell Madame N'Dour's lilac perfume before he ever saw her. She came in the shop almost every morning, pretending to keep a watchful eye on her competition, but what she really wanted was Mamadou to come run her grocery store. She owned three or four businesses in Little Senegal, and Mamadou had a reputation for being trustworthy, a family man. Madame N'Dour was tiny and round; she wore silver earrings and big sunglasses that gave her the regal air of a queen bee. She stood by the window and ran her withered hand over a crate filled with bananas and oranges. "Monsieur Talib," she said, picking up an orange. "You call this fruit?"

Talib puffed his chest. "And what do you call it?"

She snorted. "I don't think I can tell you what I call it," she said. "Not out loud." She dumped the orange back into the crate, wiping her hands together like she had just run them through mud. She took a few steps towards the stand-up coolers in the back—as a rule, she liked to torture Talib at least twice when she came in—but instead she made a detour and ambled up to the counter, lowering her shades to look right into Mamadou's eyes. "Why do you waste your time here? You should come work for me, run my shop," she said. "I'll pay you double whatever your uncle pays you."

"You realize I pay him a fortune," Talib said. "We are talking a great deal of money."

"He is *worth* a fortune," she said, as if they were discussing someone on television or a character in a book, not a man standing right in front of them. She pretended to turn and look at the phone card display. "He has a reputation for honesty. But you forget, I know exactly how much you pay him. Your wife and I play cards together, and I let her win."

"Perhaps," Talib said, pulling on the end of his shaggy beard. "But you see, Madame, my nephew also has a dark secret."

Mamadou rolled his tired eyes. "Uncle, please."

Madame N'Dour peered at Mamadou a second time, as if searching the surface of a precious stone for a deeper flaw she might have missed before. "Secret?" She took a step backwards and closed one eye, still staring. "What secret?"

"You see," Talib whispered, leaning closer. "My nephew secretly wants to be a *poet*."

Her wrinkled face suddenly turned sour. "A poet? I don't need a poet."

Talib's belly shook when he laughed. "But why not?"

"Because poets are dreamers," she said. "And dreamers are no good with money."

"Madame N'Dour," Mamadou said. "I can easily run your grocery and help my uncle here at the same time. I will be back in two days. I can come by your shop then and we can work out the details if you wish." He felt his uncle's stare but offered the old woman a warm smile.

"I will expect you," she said, nodding. "And where are you going for two days?"

"The desert," he said. "Sometimes I like to go there alone, to clear my head."

"And write your poetry," she added. "As long as you keep the poetry out in the desert, we will get along fine."

"Wait, what about me?" Talib said, beating his soft chest. "Who will talk to the damned lottery computer when it refuses to work? Who will remind me to stir my *yaasa* so it does not simmer too long? Who will taste my *ceebu yapp* over and over to make sure it is perfect?"

Madame N'Dour waved a hand at his fat belly. "It seems you are well qualified."

Mamadou smiled for the first time that day, putting his arm around his uncle's thick shoulders. "You mean, who will do all the work around here so you can drink Red Vine with the other old revolutionaries and tell your dusty stories about Dakar," he said, laughing. "Don't worry, uncle, there is enough of me to go around. And besides, Fatima and Zayne are both getting old enough. They can come help you after school."

"I don't want girls working in this shop," Talib said, waving his hands in the air. "Even if they *are* your daughters. I'll never be able to tell jokes again. The good ones, anyway."

Madame N'Dour raised the back of her palm to her forehead. "The world will crumble from the loss." She snorted again and turned to leave. "Then I will see you Monday, Mamadou. Best to your Isha and the girls. And good luck with your—poetry."

"Thank you, Madame," Mamadou said. "I will write one for you."

She was halfway out the door when she stopped and turned around. "You know, a customer once tried to pay me with a poem. He tried to convince me that the words he had written for me on a piece of paper were worth something. Do you believe that? After he had already eaten half a box of cookies."

"What did you do?" Talib said.

"What do you think? I called the police." With that, she slipped out the door.

When she was long gone, Talib came over and leaned on the counter to hiss at his nephew, see-sawing back and forth on the balls of his feet. "Oh, what a traitor you are. *Thank you, Madame N'Dour. Yes, Madame N'Dour.* Just see if I let you take any of my food with you to the desert."

Mamadou pulled his weekend backpack from where he stored it under the counter. "Usually I just pack some power bars and few bottles of water. Along with books."

Talib shook his head. "How can a man write poetry on cardboard and water?"

Mamadou ignored him and looked around, thinking of what he had to do before he could leave. "I will stock the coolers before I go," he said, snapping his fingers. "On a warm day like this, you will sell a lot of cold drinks."

"This is Arizona," Talib said. "It is always warm. Even now, in November."

Mamadou knew that if he stood still, he would have a lecture coming about how *it may be hot here, but no place on earth is hotter than Senegal*, so he quickly jogged towards the curtain that separated the shop from the back room. "And uncle, if you can find the deposit bag on that mess you call a desk before I leave, I will stop at the bank."

Talib smiled as he watched his nephew disappear into the back. He helped himself to a peppermint as he listened to him rummaging around the stacks of soda and beer. "So this is where it all starts," Talib yelled, loud enough for Mamadou to hear.

A few moments later, Mamadou came out lugging two cases of Coca-Cola, heading for the stand-ups in the rear of the store. "What are you talking about? What is starting?"

"You," Talib said. "*You* are starting. Yesterday you ran a corner shop. Today you run two shops. Who knows what you'll be doing tomorrow."

"Stop making fun," Mamadou said, putting down the heavy load with a clank against the concrete floor and ripping open the top box. He opened one of the coolers and started to make room for the six-packs. "The truth is, I am almost forty years old. Isha and I can use the money."

"I am being serious," the old man said, a hint of sentiment seeping into his graveled voice. He walked over to the coolers and stood over his nephew as he worked. "Me, I am happy to be where I am—an old man who has already seen his share of the world. An old cook who knows he will die here. But you," he said, putting his finger into his nephew's chest. "The world has plans for you, I have no doubt. Your mother and father knew it, too. I just want you to realize you are someone special."

"I think you are the one who has simmered on the burner too long. The heat from the stove has made you crazy." Mamadou started to break down the empty boxes.

"You are driving out to the desert to write poems," Talib said. "And you call me crazy."

Two miles east of Tortilla Flat, Arizona 88 turned to packed dirt and dust as it wound along the Salt River through the north spur of the Superstitions. Mamadou loved that moment when his tires left the smooth pavement and started to spit gravel; it reminded him that he was crossing into a different world, one that didn't rely on cash registers and balance sheets. He had been driving out to the mountains for years, to read and to write poems and to think without all the distractions of a civilized life. Isha used to wonder if her husband's desert retreats were simply an excuse for something else more sinister, but after the first time he came home crusted with dirt and smelling like sweat, she stopped worrying.

He knew the range was a magical place. The Apache and Pima believed there was a cave deep in the Superstitions that would lead to the bottom of the world. And it was also the home of the elusive Lost Dutchman Mine which had attracted amateur treasure hunters for more than a hundred years. Mamadou liked to avoid the well-worn trails that snaked their way through the valleys here, preferring to weave his own path between the saguaro and prickly pear that dotted the landscape. This time out, he planned on hiking the length of La Barge Canyon, up and over Battleship, and then make the short climb up the north face of Montana de Luz to find his favorite hiding place. It had been said the Spanish conquistador Coronado saw it from a distance and named it *La Montaña de Luz*, the mountain of light, because when the morning sun shone on its east face, the painted rock exploded into an array of colors. There was a small cave near the top of the mountain, a natural staircase carved into the stone leading up to a cramped grotto about fifteen feet long and five feet wide, the perfect place for a poet to decompress from the world.

It was about an hour before sunset when he reached the foot of La Montaña de Luz. He took a drink from a water bottle and steeled himself for the last climb. When he made it to the cave he would rest his legs and eat some food by lamplight before reading; he had brought Plato's *Republic* and a new book of poems by a Chicano writer he admired. He started to scramble up the loose rock, using his hands for balance on the steep grade, when he heard a strange noise ahead. At first he thought it was a trick of the wind, but now he was sure of it: there was music coming from above. He looked around, thinking it might be an echo from another hiker's radio, but he could see nothing moving on the horizon. Mamadou clambered the last hundred yards up to the cave entrance and peered up the steps into the dim.

There was music coming from the cave, *his* cave. It sounded like a lone trumpet.

He crept into the cave and saw a man sitting on a rock, blowing his horn. He wore the clothes of another time: bowler hat, double-breasted suit, black and white wingtip shoes that had been rubbed to a brilliant shine. Mamadou wondered if he'd hit his head and was transported to some sort of dream, but the cave looked exactly the same as he remembered it.

The trumpet player stopped suddenly when he noticed his visitor.

Mamadou took a step back. "I'm sorry, I did not mean to disturb. I was just listening."

"Why not come and sit a spell," the man said, motioning him to sit down to a flat rock. "You made it this far, you must be tired. My name's Gabriel," he said. "Some folks just call me Jib. You know, like the sail."

"That music you were playing," Mamadou said. "It was very beautiful."

"Thank you kindly," Jib said, bowing a little. "It's an old one, that's for sure. I've had plenty of practice on it. Do you play?"

"No," he said, sitting down. "I never had the talent for music. I write poetry."

"Well, that's music, ain't it? I never liked music without words to go with it. Take that song I was just playing. It's got words to it—more verses than I can count. No lie, no lie. You want to hear a little of it?"

Mamadou nodded.

"Okay," Gabriel said, licking his lips and settling his fingertips back onto the valves. "Here goes nothing." He drew a deep breath and blew into the mouthpiece, playing a few notes from the song he was playing before. Then he lowered his trumpet to his knee and sang a line of the song in the same melody. His voice echoed against the cave walls, a lullaby of beauty and sadness. He only sang for a few seconds, but Mamadou already thought it was the most magnificent poem he'd ever heard; he felt a tear welling in his eye as he listened.

"Now it's your turn," Gabriel said. "Ready to sing along?"

"I can't," Mamadou said. "I don't know the words."

"I'll teach them to you. You got something to write with?"

"My notebook," Mamadou said, patting his knapsack. "To write down my poems."

"Perfect. Go ahead and get your notebook out. We've got a lot of work to do."

Mamadou hurried to unzip the top of his bag; he rummaged inside for his little spiral diary and a pen. He was excited, the way a schoolboy feels when he's learning something for the first time. He pulled out the book and flipped to an empty page. He uncapped the pen and held it above the page; he was about to write down the song's title at the top, but he realized Jib never mentioned it to him. "What is the name of the song?"

"That's for you to decide," Jib said. He drew a little closer, looking Mamadou right in the eye. "Listen, poets are the creators," he said, jabbing his finger at the empty page of the notebook. "Poets are the true namers of things. Now, you ready?"

Mamadou nodded eagerly; he liked the idea of a poet as a maker, an architect of useful things the world could not do without. He liked the notion that a poem could be important, its language becoming law, its words becoming more than mere words. He wanted to believe in a God that was first and foremost a poet, a creator of beautiful things.

Gabriel licked his lips again and raised up his horn. "Okay, here we go. Now I need you to listen carefully." The last rays of the setting sun were draining out of the cave as the two men huddled together. "You need to write every one of these words down."

Tommy Zurhellen was born in New York City. With assistance from the GI Bill, he earned an MFA in Fiction at the University of Alabama in 2002 and since then his short fiction has appeared widely in literary magazines such as *Carolina Quarterly, Appalachee Review* and *Quarterly West. Apostle Islands* is his second novel, following *Nazareth, North Dakota* (Atticus Books, 2011) which began the allegorical account of Sam Davidson, a modern-day messiah. His latest project is a travel memoir titled *Tales from the VFW* where Tommy will visit Veterans of Foreign Wars (VFW) posts across the globe, recording the vital stories and memories of our American war veterans. Currently he teaches at Marist College in upstate New York, where he also serves as Director of the Creative Writing program.

To learn more about Tommy Zurhellen and other Atticus authors, visit the Atticus Books website at:
atticusbooksonline.com.

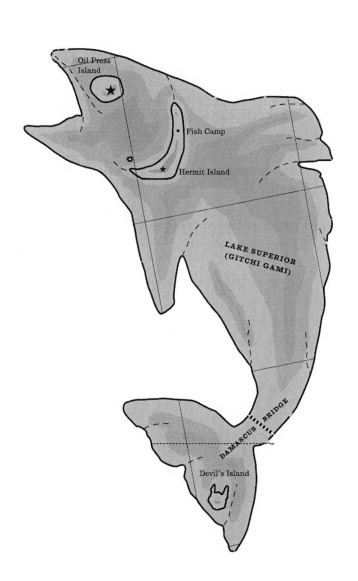

Oil Press
Island

Fish Camp

Hermit Island

LAKE SUPERIOR
(GITCHI GAMI)

DAMASCUS BRIDGE

Devil's Island

A Note About Lake Superior

Lake Superior is the largest freshwater lake in the world. Originally named *Gitchi Gami* or "big water" by the Chippewa, generations of fishermen and sailors have since come to know it as "the lake that never gives up its dead" due to its extreme depth of over 1,300 feet and frigid water temperatures that hover just above freezing year-round. During the 17th Century, French settlers found the chain of twenty-two islands that snake off the northern tip of what is now Wisconsin and named them *Les Apotres*, or the Apostles. Since 1970, all these remote islands with names like Hermit, Oak, Eagle and Manitou have been designated as a National Lakeshore except for the largest, Madeline, which is inhabited year-round. One of the outermost islands was named Devil's Island because of the eerie, unworldly moaning sound that issues from its natural caves when waves roll in and out. The stretch of open water above the Apostles is commonly known as The Graveyard, due to the numerous shipwrecks that are scattered along its rocky bottom. Since the early 1800s, the southern rim of Lake Superior has been a busy shipping lane between Duluth in the west and Sault Ste. Marie in the east, and hundreds of boats and ships have been lost here, along with hundreds of lives. The most famous of these is the SS *Edmund Fitzgerald*, a 729-foot ore freighter which was split in half by a storm in 1975 and later immortalized in the Gordon Lightfoot song "The Wreck of the Edmund Fitzgerald." The lake is home to a wide variety of fish and birds, and sightings of a sea monster named "Pressie" (after Presque Isle, where it has been spotted) are nothing new; the Chippewa have legends of an enormous spiked catlike beast called Mishipishu that prowls the shoreline.

A Note About the Apostles

The word apostle comes from the old Greek word *apostolos*, which means "one who is sent away." According to both New Testament and apocryphal accounts, the apostles spread out over the known world after Jesus' death and resurrection, preaching the Word and performing many miracles of their own. Generally regarded as Jesus' closest confidante, **Mary Magdelene** was the first to see Jesus risen from the dead, although she did not recognize him at first, thinking he was simply a gardener working near the open tomb. She escaped capture by authorities in Palestine (along with her brother Lazarus and sister Martha) by setting sail in a boat "with no sail or rudder" and landing at the busy seaport of Marseille, in what is now France. To evade arrest there by Roman forces, Mary Magdelene hid alone in a cave deep in the hardscrabble Var mountains outside the city. She then befriended a local farmer named Maximilian, who was at her side for the remainder of her life until her death at the age of fifty. In the 12th Century, the Count D'Anjou located and exhumed her bones and placed them in a tomb under a specially-built Basilica in the nearby village of Saint-Maximin-la-Sainte-Baume, where her sarcophagus can still be viewed by the public today. **Peter** (literally, "the Rock" in Greek) along with his brother **Andrew** originally owned a fishing company on the Sea of Galilee where a number of the other apostles worked for them, such as **James the Lesser** and his brother **John**, whom Jesus nicknamed the "Sons of Thunder" due to their outspoken and rambunctious nature. After Jesus' death, Peter was thrown into prison but miraculously escaped with the help of angels. According to legend, he was recaptured by the Roman Emperer Nero in AD 64 and died by crucifixion in Rome during the Great Fire. Although he infamously denied knowing Jesus three times during his arrest and trial, Peter worked tirelessly later in life as the fearless leader of the nascent Christian community and is considered to be the first Pope. Saint Mark, Peter's cellmate while in prison, is credited with recording Peter's memories into the first gospel, the Gospel of Mark. The apostle **Junia** is only mentioned once in the New Testament, but since this is almost certainly a woman's name, her inclusion among the male apostles has stirred a great deal of debate over the centuries. **Thomas** Didymus (literally, "the twin" in Greek) reportedly traveled as far as India to preach the Word and there he established the "Seven and a Half Churches" in what is now known as the province of Keralam. Annual festivals are devoted to him there, even today. **Judas** reportedly was in charge of the group's finances and was later given the added name Iscariot due to his suspected allegiance to a notorious group called *Sicarii* ("Dagger Men") who were Jewish zealots dedicated to the independence of Judea from the Roman Empire. His death is the subject of several differing accounts, including one of tormented suicide, but the most well-known may come from the Acts of the Apostles where Judas buys a small farm on the outskirts of Jerusalem with the thirty talents of silver given him for betraying Jesus, only to split his head open on a rock while working the field. To this day the field is called *Akeldama*, or "Field of Blood." Finally, **Paul** of Tarsus is considered to be an apostle although he never actually met Jesus in person; in fact, he was dedicated to the capture and persecution of early Christians until his own conversion on the Damascus road, where he was thrown from his horse and blinded for three days. Originally named Saul and born a Roman citizen, he slowly regained his sight through the kindness of the Christian named Ananias who found him and took him in. He then changed his name to Paul and spent the rest of his life building the foundations of what would become the Roman Catholic Church, through his encouraging letters and constant visits to new converts in scattered communities like Thessaloniki and Galatia. He often argued bitterly with **James the Greater**, Jesus' stepbrother, on the inclusion of non-Jews into the fledgling faith. Like his compatriot Peter, Paul was eventually imprisoned by Emperor Nero and subsequently martyred, although his Roman citizenship accorded him a death by beheading instead of crucifixion, which was reserved as the most dire punishment for enemies of the state at that time.